THE MYSTERY OF THE WETTEST WEDDING EVER

A Lady Darriby-Jones Mystery

CM RAWLINS

CleanTales Publishing

Copyright © CleanTales Publishing

First published in January 2025

All characters and events in this publication, other than those clearly in the public domain, are fictitious and any resemblance to real persons, living or dead, is purely coincidental.

Copyright © CleanTales Publishing

The moral right of the author has been asserted.

All rights reserved. This book or any portion thereof may not be reproduced or used in any manner whatsoever without the express written permission of the publisher except for the use of brief quotations in a book review.

For questions and comments about this book, please contact info@cleantales.com

ISBN: 9798308021131
Imprint: Independently Published

Other books in the A Lady Darriby-Jones Mystery series

The Mystery of the Polite Man

The Mystery of the American Slug

The Mystery of the Back Passage

The Mystery of the Murder that Wasn't

The Mystery of Miss Cess Pitt

The Mystery of the Bag of Bones

The Mystery of the Sudden Demotion

The Mystery of the Missing Misses

The Mystery of the Royal Rogue

The Mystery of Mothering Sunday

The Mystery of the Christmas Crackers

The Mystery of the Wettest Wedding Ever

A Lady Darriby-Jones Mystery

BOOK TWELVE

Chapter One

"Why the rush, my dear?"

"Mummy, this is my wedding and I want to do it my way. I just don't want to delay the event a moment longer than it needs to be."

"It's not...?"

"No, Mummy, it's not. I just want to be Lady Alice Burrows."

"The problem is Lord Fork, of course," Lady Darriby-Jones replied, wondering again why she and Darriby had gone for him as Alice's godfather. He was an absolute gentleman, spilling over with integrity and generosity.

It's just that, as an explorer and self-confessed adventurer, the man was seldom around in the tamer-than-tame British Isles. There was far too much to occupy him in other, vastly more exciting corners of the world.

"I've sent him a telegram," Lady Alice replied, "so he bally well better be with us on the day." She stopped a moment, then asked if one could divorce one's godfather for non-attendance at critical events in one's life.

"I don't think so, my dear, otherwise there'd be a regular exchange for unwanted godparents."

"You mean like the stock exchange, Mummy?"

"Yes, that's what I was thinking, where you trade the one you don't want for someone you do want, thus making you happy and, presumably, the other party to the transaction equally delighted."

"Well, I do love Lord Knife," Lady Alice said, using the ages-old nickname for him, "but he is 'cutting' it a bit fine, don't you think?"

"Very good, Ali," Lady Darriby-Jones replied, "although if you speak too ill of him, he may 'cut' you out of his will."

"Ah, well, Mummy, I must say your wit is 'knife-edge sharp' today. But seriously, I would like the wedding as soon as it poss can be managed, because, having said I never wanted to marry, I now so want to be joined to Mr Alfred Burrows, that I just can't wait a moment longer than I have to."

"Well, Mr Clambers will be with us later this afternoon and we can discuss it all with him."

"Did you use Clambers and Mason when you got married?" Lady Alice asked. Lady Darriby-Jones replied that it hadn't been so fashionable to have wedding organisers before the war.

"Besides," she said thoughtfully, "we were in a hurry too, but not for the reason you might think. Daddy, your grandfather, was dying and he'd worked so hard to get the marriage between your father and me arranged. We all desperately wanted him to see it happen. That meant a reasonably quick and quiet wedding, just the local people and a few handfuls who could travel at short notice. I don't think we had more than two hundred guests in total."

"When did he die, Mummy?" Lady Alice asked, having heard the story countless times over the last two decades, but still enjoying the facts as much as ever.

"The day after we got back from our honeymoon," Lady Darriby-Jones, "it was so sad. As if he was hanging on to check the wedding had really taken place and only let go when he saw the evidence laid out before him."

"Is that when you introduced him to Torino?" Again, the question had been asked, and answered, many times before.

"Yes, Torino stowed away on the boat we were on, having followed us all the way up France on the way back. Now, Mr Clambers will be here shortly. Why don't you go and..."?

"Put on a pretty dress? Yes, I'll do that this moment. I love you, Mummy."

The door to her private sitting room opened and closed again, leaving the kiss still lingering on Lady Darriby-Jones' lips. To this day, she couldn't understand the changes love had brought to Lady Alice. Of old she had been acerbic and vitriolic, if you could have both in the same bottle, certainly she used to frown out her sarcasm. Then, just like that, she had switched to sweetness and light.

All because of love.

They met Mr Clambers in the library, where most of the business of the estate was discussed and plans made. Darriby put in an appearance, something Lady Darriby-Jones had known he would do, despite his reputation for missing important occurrences.

When it came to his daughter, her husband could be relied upon.

Lady Darriby-Jones knew Mr Clambers slightly, but nothing had prepared her for the surprise she received when he walked into the library, announced in impeccable fashion by Torino, who managed to incorporate formality with his warm Italian accent in a magical mix that he well and truly owned. The same couldn't be said for Mr Clambers, however. He was almost wild with reddened cheeks and dark eyes as if he'd been through some tremendous ordeal, and only just came out the right side of it.

Of course, Lady Darriby-Jones was too polite to question what happened, but her interest was immediately raised. He looked like he had just come from ten rounds in the ring with Jack Dempsey, not that anyone would survive ten rounds with Jack. She had seen him fight once in New York and could still picture his competitor's face.

Mr Clambers, while not actually cut or bleeding, looked as harrowed as the man who had stood up to JD in New York.

She may have been too polite to ask for a reason for his disturbed state, but Mr Clambers clearly felt a need to explain.

"Good afternoon, Lady Darriby-Jones and Lord Darriby. It's very nice to see you both again and congratulations to Lady Alice, too." So far, nothing out of the ordinary, but then the truth broke out. "You see me rather the worse for wear," he said, "a whisky perhaps, and I could tell you all about it?"

So far, so good, thought Lady Darriby-Jones. As to the cause, it could easily be a scuffle on the train with somebody of equivalent stature to the champion boxer.

Or perhaps he had walked into a door. Well, if that was the case, he must have walked into several doors in quick succession, suffering considerable shell shock from the impact, too.

Then, his tale diverged from the norm, completely and utterly. "I came down on the train with Miss Mason," he said.

"How is Lucy?" Lady Alice asked. Her disastrous few weeks at a boarding school in Kent had put Alice and Lucy together. It had been a little like putting two prize bulls in the same field, although they had developed a certain amount of respect for each other, in between the interminable scrapping.

Memories of the reports Lady Darriby-Jones used to receive about the latest squabble, over ownership of a whip or a bridle usually, came back to her at that moment.

"She's in fine form, Lady Alice, although she and I haven't exactly hit it off recently."

"And that's why you're looking a little the worse for wear?"

"Exactly, Lady Darriby-Jones. I'm afraid she got to me one time too many and I had sharp words with her. Do you know what the little angel did? She pushed me off the platform at Oxford station. I fell right onto the tracks and did this to myself. Still, nothing a stiff whisky and a hot bath won't put right."

Darriby, usually so remote, occupied by thoughts of his precious slugs, turned in his chair towards Torino and asked the butler to serve, "some of that excellent stuff you found in the old cellar just the other day."

"Of course, my lord."

The twenty-year-old Scotch helped to revive Mr Clambers from his shock, as did the roaring fire, acting upon his shaken temperament. Within minutes of the first sip, Mr Clambers was heading back towards his usual joviality, warming himself by the fire, and by the very ordinary, plain comfort of the library.

But much to Lady Darriby-Jones' annoyance, as he returned from the near-dead, he retreated from full disclosure, talking instead about their plans for the wedding. Lady Darriby-Jones wondered whether she would ever be able to extricate herself from his constant flow of chit mixed with chat; her irritation with this stream of words made her determined to try.

"Is that a yawn, I detect, Mr Clambers? I've kept you pinned down with my incessant gaggling. Let me make amends by ordering you that bath you thought you might require. There's plenty of time this evening and in the morning to discuss all our plans. Right now, you need a hot bath before changing for supper." Before he could object, Torino was at the door, decanter in hand, judging a refill might sway the balance, thus giving Lady Darriby-Jones a little peace. Mr Clambers was, indeed, ready for a bath and, being the talkative type, said as much several times over.

How many times did she wish to High Heaven that events that day, night and into the next day had taken a slightly different turn? There are those who argue that one tiny moment of hesitation, indecision or, even, the relentless pursuit of objectives by the confident person can truly influence every subsequent action or scene.

Lady Darriby-Jones wasn't one of those types, preferring the notion of a broad sweep of events that you might be able to influence, but could not alter. After supper, Mr Clambers had asked for a key to one of the outside doors, so he could explore outside a little, despite the gloom of the February night.

Those who heard him ask for the key later assumed he had returned and gone to bed. Those who hadn't heard, just imagined him the early-to-bed type. Nobody missed poor Mr Clambers until breakfast time the next morning. Then, they imagined he had overslept and probably best to leave him be. It was only when tummies started thinking of elevenses that concerns began to emerge because there was neither sight nor sound of the affable wedding arranger.

Then, Cess came into the house, breathing furiously. "Help," she cried, "help, he's murdered, pinned to a tree by an arrow."

"Who?" Lady Darriby-Jones wanted to know.

"Why, Mr Clambers, of course. It's absolutely awful, Aunty."

Chapter Two

"Pinned to a side of a tree, you say?" Lady Darriby-Jones asked, the breath quite taken from her.

"Yes," Cess replied, "pierced through the heart and held by the arrow up against that giant tree. You know, the huge yew on the way to the Dowager House. It looks like he's just standing there. Oh," she continued, having trouble in describing the vividness of what she had experienced, "you see, the arrow pierced through his heart and pinned him against the tree. What on earth happened, you say? Aunty, I saw it with my own eyes! Mrs Robinson and I were getting some fresh air between the bouts of rain, going over my chemistry revision. Is this to be another mystery? What will Freddie say, having missed it all? He's not coming for a few days. What rotten timing. Why on earth did this gentleman choose a day to get murdered without Freddie being here?"

"Cess," said Mrs Robinson, her mother, officially her tutor too, "really, the insensitive things you say. The poor man's been murdered and you're more concerned about..."

"Mummy," Cess replied, forgetting the convention of calling her mother 'Mrs Robinson' during school hours, "it's just a dead body now. There's no point in getting all het-up about it. It's for the police to examine and determine the cause of death. Well, you see, the cause of death might seem pretty obvious, but you never know what else there might be to discover." Cess was losing herself in her excitement; it had long been her dream to become a pathologist after qualifying as a doctor. But first she had to gain admission to the university and she had proved herself relentless in her determination to achieve student status, working hard at her schoolwork every day, yet, somehow, retaining the love of life that emanated from every pore of her body.

But all this was lost to Lady Darriby-Jones; she heard the words, processed them at some level, but remained non-responsive, with her mind completely elsewhere, roaming around in the past, seeking connections with the present.

An arrow through the heart.
Pinned to a tree.
Where had she heard that before?

She could hear the voice relaying the story, just could not quite place it; it danced just outside her recognition, teasing whatever section of the brain handled memories.

What could she count on? The voice had been much younger, indicating it was a long time ago. The speaker had authority, but with an English accent rather than a Welsh one.

Lady Darriby-Jones had never been to England before the wedding preparation discussions at... at Darriby Hall.

Did that mean?

Yes, it had to be. The story about the arrow and the tree had to be connected to Darriby, making it a huge coincidence to have another story about an arrow and a tree surface right now.

Or was it coincidence? She was on the fence about coincidences generally, wondering whether there was any truth in the old detective maxim that there was no such thing as a coincidence.

A decidedly English accent. Darriby spoke with the soft Scottish blur he inherited from his mother who had grown up in a huge and ancient leaky castle somewhere in Argyll, set back at the end of a long sea loch in which seals abounded.

Who else had spoken to her on that very first trip to Darriby? She went back over the events of two decades earlier. Many people had sent smiles her way, but few had broken out to use their voice. She traced back through her memory of that journey.

That was it.

"Torino, have Smith meet us by the giant yew, if you'd be so kind."

"Certainly, milady."

Smith had told her the story. Now, she would question him as to how much he could remember over twenty years later.

. . .

"Certainly, milady, I know the old tale very well indeed. There are remarkable..."

"Tell it to me, now, if you'd be so kind, Smith." It wasn't often that Lady Darriby-Jones interrupted, having had the very best manners instilled in her from a young age.

But, she considered, by way of excuse for her actions, there was a time and a place for everything. And now was a time for disregarding convention and going out on a limb.

"Well, milady, it goes back to the very origin of the name Darriby. The story goes that the first Darriby came over with William the Conqueror and..."

"No, Smith."

"No, milady?" Smith sounded surprised. "I thought you wanted..."

Lady Darriby-Jones stepped in once more, making it a trio of interruptions that afternoon. "No, think, Smith, tell it to me like you did almost twenty-two years ago."

"Well," he said, "it was like this." He cleared his throat and continued his tale in his younger voice, while Lady Darriby-Jones felt twenty-two years fall away, disappearing like the tide going out:

Like so much at the time, the coming of William the Conqueror changed everything. Jean d'Arribé was one of those who came across from Normandy and impressed William at the Battle of Hastings and in subsequent efforts to subdue the country of

England. Not only a brave soldier, he was a good administrator as well. He had no estate in Normandy, hence everything to gain by coming over here.

The new king settled some land on him at the beginning of 1067, specifically we believe it to be the home farm to the Darriby estate, on which he built a tiny manor house, the ruins of which form the steadings of home farm. Jean, the story goes, had an intended wife back in Normandy, chosen by his father, also a soldier of fortune but too old to come across with the invasion. However, Jean and his fiancé had made a private pact not to wed if they could help it, because they disliked each other as children. Jean thought marrying a local was an excellent way of getting out of the wedding scheduled for later that year in Normandy.

His own choice of bride was a love match, because the story was she was stunningly attractive and had a lovely personality. Her name was Arundel and her father had been dispossessed of the land, subsequently granted to Jean. They married on a cold winter's day in early March 1067. Apparently, it poured with rain all day and Jean's mother was furious. She stayed in the manor house and refused to attend the wedding at what later became Darriby Church. She cursed the union, her heart set on her son's marriage to Matilda back in Normandy, saying every winter wedding at Darriby would be equally set to end in disaster.

This union between Jean and Arundel did end in disaster, but at first, it seemed the curse had no force. A son was born just before Christmas 1067. He was to become the first Lord Darriby, although it was still spelt in French fashion for quite some years to come. He became a Gentleman of the King's Chamber to Henry I, one of the sons of William the Conqueror. From there, he became an instrumental figure in Anglo-Norman politics and also led various military expeditions while increasing his landholding around Darriby considerably. Incidentally, it's worth noting that no Darriby has ever sold land on the home estate. They've speculated on land in other areas of the country, but have only ever added to the holdings they have here in Oxfordshire.

Arundel was a great archer, something unusual for women at that time, mainly because of the strength required to pull the long bow, which was increasingly becoming the bow of choice in England. However, she, so the story goes, could handle a long bow with ease and could also make bows and arrows herself. She hunted almost daily, bringing much fresh meat to the table. That's why the freeze above the door at Darriby Hall has an archer's bow and a quiver of arrows. People think it's to do with Cupid, but it stems from Arundel the Archer as she came to be known.

It was on their first wedding anniversary that disaster struck. They say she was out hunting early one day and did not return for breakfast. Jean organised a search party and led it himself, seeking all around. You have to remember that the woods were far more prevalent in those days, much like Darriby Wood is today, up on Arundel Hill, of course, named after the first lady of Darriby. It was hard to search everywhere because of the dense undergrowth, while the trees made it hard to see with clarity.

Eventually, however, they found her, pinned by an arrow through her heart to a giant yew tree. She was quite dead, had been for quite some time and nobody ever discovered who had murdered her.

There is a quaint sequel to this story. Jean grieved for quite some time after this. He neglected his responsibilities and stopped caring for anything. His parents were too old and infirm to come from Normandy, but Matilda, his original intended, did make the journey about three years later.

Despite their past, they fell in love during the course of her stay at Darriby and were married in the church here. They both lived for a long time and were happy ever after, just like something written as a fairy story. The match was childless, but Matilda Darriby took young Jean, Arundel's son, as her own and loved him without question.

"So," said Lady Darriby-Jones, "that's why every heir to Darriby ever after has been named Jean. My husband, the current Lord Darriby, was a second son, but took the name when his older brother died."

"Exactly, milady, and here's where the body is, just as the first Jean must have found his wife all those years ago."

Lady Darriby-Jones looked to where Smith pointed and saw the body of Mr Clambers pinned to the yew tree with an arrow through his heart.

History was repeating itself. Could two murders nine centuries apart be connected in some strange way?

Chapter Three

The police had to be called, of course, and that meant the presence of one of Lady Darriby-Jones' least favourite people, that being Detective Chief Inspector Rory 'Rude' Manners. Occupying a rank, in her opinion, far too high for his natural abilities, she suspected he had been promoted over the years not on merit, but to move him on, to make him somebody else's problem.

She had heard from Darriby of such happenings in the army during the war, but had never approved of the practice, despite the fact that she knew she was guilty of similar in moving household staff around rather than biting the bullet and getting rid of the offending individual.

And DCI Manners was definitely offending in the sense that he was lazy, unscrupulous and downright rude. However, he was also the senior police officer at the Darriby station, which covered all the surrounding villages, making for quite a territory for the odious man to rule over.

He arrived at the scene shortly after Lady Darriby-Jones, trailing a small corps of uniformed officers behind him, like royal attendants or bridesmaids at a wedding. At least Sergeant Maeve Morgan was one of them, a fellow Cardiffian and a good friend to Lady Darriby-Jones since their somewhat unsettled introduction to each other a few years earlier.

His arrival usually caused immense disruption and, as Lady Darriby-Jones observed, this time was no different.

"What have we got here, then?" he said in a tone reminiscent of the old musical hall policemen she remembered from her Cardiff childhood. It just lacked the 'hello, hello, hello' at the start.

"A dead body, Mr Manners," said Cess, not hiding the disdain from her voice.

"I know that, Miss Pitt. I wasn't born yesterday, you know."

Lady Darriby-Jones was pleased at Freddie's absence; she knew he took unkindly to anyone speaking disrespectfully to his beloved Cess; if present, he would have confronted the police detective head on about his lack of manners.

"It's a gentleman, sir," one of the policemen offered, meaning to make a distinction between the classes, but Manners took it the wrong way, declaring that he knew full well a male of the species when confronted with one.

Lady Darriby-Jones wondered why anyone working for Manners ever volunteered any information his way; all that happened in response was a ritual head being bitten off, usually accompanied by a few choice words of derision.

"I know who the gentleman is," she offered, stressing the word 'gentleman' in a way that would point out the policeman's distinction clearly enough.

"I directed my question towards my officers, Lady Darriby."

"Jones."

"What?"

"The name is Lady Darriby-Jones, Mr Manners. Do I go around the place calling you Mr Mann? No, well, I would appreciate a little common politeness."

"As I said, Lady Darriby, my question wasn't pointed your way." Then Manners contradicted the stand he'd taken by asking Lady Darriby-Jones for details of who the person was.

Or had been at one time, for he was very dead.

"His name is Mr Clambers of the London firm of wedding planners, Clambers and Mason. He was visiting us to determine arrangements for the wedding of my daughter, Lady Alice, to Mr Alfred Burrows."

"I hope I'm going to get an invitation."

"We didn't get as far as the guest list, Mr Manners," Lady Darriby-Jones replied, with sufficient frostiness to get her point across. "And now, we never will, at least not with Mr Clambers, at any rate."

This is when Lady Darriby-Jones made her mistake. Manners examined the body, shuffling around the huge yew tree a few times, stroking his chin and pulling at his moustache, both actions designed to make him look studious and all-seeing.

"Looks like a professional job," he said at long last. "Harris, go and check the Darriby Archery Club for any missing bows and arrows."

"Sir," said Harris, jumping from foot to foot, a little like a schoolboy denied the chance to visit the toilet.

"I just gave you an instruction, didn't I?"

"Yes, sir, but..."

"'But' is a word I'd have stricken from the dictionary in a heartbeat," the inspector replied. "I don't want to hear any 'buts' to my orders. Is that clear?"

"But sir," Maeve tried to speak up, intervening to protect her colleague, no doubt. "I think it's imperative you hear Harris out. He has important..."

"Go, now, Harris. Orders are to be obeyed, full stop. Unless you want to be up on a charge of insubordination?"

Harris left, leaving a gap, not so much in a physical sense, but in an awkward moment. Maeve tried to catch the inspector's attention, but he seemed resolved to avoid all contact, continuing to look at the body pinned to the tree.

Until a voice Lady Darriby-Jones recognised rolled across the clearing where they had gathered.

"Mr Inspector – I don't know your name – what your nice police officer was trying to tell you just now is that he has a very good idea where the bow comes from."

This, at long last, got Manners' attention.

"Who are you and what do you mean?" he asked, adding that his name was Detective Chief Inspector Manners, a senior position in the police force.

"I'm Lucy Mason and, if you'd allow me to come through your dratted cordon, I could, in all likelihood, confirm to you within seconds where that bow belongs. You see, I think it is mine."

The police cordon separated without Manners' instruction, just like the Red Sea had done for Moses. Lady Darriby-Jones took the opportunity to accompany her friend Lucy Mason to the crime scene.

"Yes," she said, "it's my bow, the one stolen this morning."

"Alright, alright, alright," Manners sounded irritated, "first things first, as I said, first things first. How do you know it's your bow? One bow of the same make must look much like another, don't you know?"

"Yes, but look at this," Lucy replied. "You see the 'L.M.' on the inside edge of the bow?"

"Lucy Mason?"

"Actually, no."

"Then it's not yours?"

"I didn't say that, did I everyone?" Lucy turned to appeal to the wider audience gathering around, gaining general approval for her stance. "What I said is that (a) it's my bow and (b) it has my initials. You confused it as standing for Lucy Mason', whereas in actual fact it stands for Lady, not Lucy."

"So, you're another of these toffs," Manners murmured, not realising that Lucy had excellent hearing.

"If being a 'toff' covers being a third cousin to the Prince of Wales, then, undoubtedly, Mr Manners, I am a 'toff'."

"Alright, so how come your bow ended up here, with an arrow straight through this person's heart?"

"I don't know, Chief Inspector, I reported my missing bow to your nice police station this morning, gave all the details to that nice PC Harris. He was trying to tell you about that just now."

"I'll run my own enquiries. Thank you, Miss Mason."

"Wrong."

"What?"

"You should have said, 'I'll run my own enquiries, thank you, Lady Mason.' It's important to get these things right. Don't you agree Lady Darriby-Jones?"

"Quite so, quite so, Lady Mason," Lady Darriby-Jones replied, wondering if this was the first time she had ever used Lucy's title in addressing her; professionally and socially, she went by the name of Lucy Mason.

"Well, there's still a lot of explaining for you to do, young lady," Manners replied, and there wasn't much fault she could find in his words this time around.

"I was camping at Barrow Long," she started, "having journeyed down on the train yesterday with Mr Clambers. I had thought about asking to stay with Lady Darriby-Jones at Darriby Hall, prior to competing at the Barrow Long

Archery Tournament over the next few days, but I had such a dreadful row with Mr Clambers that I..."

"So, you did now, did you? Have a row, I mean. That's very interesting, young lady."

"Yes, but not so..."

"I think you had better come along with me to the station."

"But I can explain..."

"Down at the station, there'll be plenty of time to explain."

"Mr Manners," put in Lady Darriby-Jones, thinking the idea that Lucy Mason, for all her idiosyncrasies and her frightful displays of temper over the years, the last person in the world to stoop to murder, "if I could just add..."

"The trouble with you, Lady Darriby, is you're always just adding little bits here and there, and they don't actually mean much other than attempts to embarrass me with the commissioner. I'd much prefer you to go back to the other side of the cordon and leave police work to the police."

"Of course, Mr Manners, I just wanted to give a character reference for Lady Mason."

"She's just helping us with our enquiries at the moment. I won't arrest her until later... I mean, may not arrest her at all."

"I think you should go, my dear," Lady Darriby-Jones said. "I'll come and see you later and can easily arrange for Mr Strawbridge, our family lawyer, to assist if necessary."

"I didn't..."

"I know you didn't, don't have the slightest suspicion, my dear girl. It's just that the police need to go through with their procedures."

"I'll make sure she's alright," whispered Maeve, having come across the clearing to escort Lucy back to the police station.

The last sight Lady Darriby-Jones had of her young friend was her being led off, back to the village for in depth questioning; she knew that, if Manners got his way, that would be the last they ever saw of Lucy.

Chapter Four

A strange thing about detective chief inspectors is that they're human, every one of them, at least partially so. They may not always appear so, but they are. Lady Darriby-Jones reminded herself of this fact as she walked back to Darriby Hall, aware that her tummy told her it was a meal time soon, but not quite sure whether it was elevenses or lunch.

Or possibly even afternoon tea. The overhung sky gave her no opportunity to gauge the state of the day from the position of the sun. In fact, it threatened more rain at any moment.

Being human was reassuring to all concerned because, in this case, it meant Manners would get tired and irritable. That meant he would storm off, either to the golf course if he had thought to put his clubs in the back of the car, or home. Either way, there would be a break in his attendance at the Darriby police station, meaning Lady Darriby-Jones could gain access, her purpose being to see, and question, Lucy.

Maeve Morgan, the enterprising police sergeant who had become a good friend to Lady Darriby-Jones, had hinted as much as she led the 'prisoner' away.

It was lunchtime and they enjoyed a game stew that went down exceedingly well. After that came the phone call.

"It's Sergeant Morgan, milady," Torino said. As far as he was concerned, he owned the telephone installed under protest a few years back, the protest being by Lady Darriby-Jones who objected to most 'new-fangled' things, on the basis that they had always got on fine without them being available. She appreciated the telephone much more these days, seeing the value of it, but still occasionally stumbled with its operation.

That's where Torino came in. There wasn't much he didn't know about telephones.

"Hello, Lady Darriby-Jones," came the warm Cardiff voice down the line, "Mr Manners has just thrown up his hands in disgust and walked out, saying he needs time to think the case through, doesn't he just?"

"Golf?"

"I saw him check his golf bag was still in the back, Lady Darriby-Jones, so I assume that to be the case, don't I? Will you come down later on?"

"No."

"No?"

"I'll come right now. I'll get Smith to drive as I don't like the look of those heavy clouds. From here," she squinted out of the window, "the big black ones look like they're hanging just over the police station."

"That's funny, Lady Darriby-Jones, because from here they look like they're right over Darriby Hall, don't they just?"

"My dear girl," Lady Darriby-Jones started, "you must try not to worry."

"The man's a brute," Lucy replied. "I mean, how else can you describe him? Ogre perhaps, or sadist?" Despite these desperate words, Lady Darriby-Jones smiled; the old fire had returned to Lucy Mason's personality.

Lady Darriby-Jones had known her since she was four-years old, liked her enormously for the direct approach she had to everything in life, a little like Cess and Freddie, she supposed. She had seen a lot of Lucy. Her father was in the colonial service and it took him abroad often. That meant she often needed somewhere to stay during school holidays when they put her in boarding school from the age of nine.

It hadn't always been a bed of roses, however. In particular, Lucy and Alice had had the fieriest of relationships, often squabbling when she came to share Darriby Hall during the holidays, much as Freddie came every holidays in the here and now.

The main problem arose when Lady Darriby-Jones made the foolish decision to attempt to get Alice an education. Alice wasn't educatable, that much should have been clear from the beginning. Instead, she put Alice into Lucy's boarding school and it was a complete disaster.

Instead of building on their friendship, they became arch enemies, neither one of them having a teaspoon of humility, and not even a salt spoon of sympathy for the other person's position. It had started with the need for Lucy to ride one of Alice's many horses she kept at school. The problem being that Lucy didn't ask, she just took it as her right.

Darriby used to joke that the sound of them arguing over in Kent could be heard all the way in Oxfordshire, adding that it upset his slugs and stopped them breeding.

A fact which, if remotely true, would actually have pleased most people living and working at Darriby Hall.

Still, Lady Darriby-Jones was immensely fond of Lucy Mason and would do anything to protect and help her.

Except, it seems, Lucy wouldn't do the simplest thing to protect herself.

"If you can tell me, Lucy dear, what you and Mr Clambers were fighting about, perhaps I can explain it to the chief inspector."

"I can't tell and won't tell. Moreover, I don't see why I should have to explain anything at all. All I need to do is to state my innocence."

"I know that to be true, my dear, but the police don't operate in that way."

"Then the police are stupid." Lady Darriby-Jones couldn't wholly disagree with that. "Well, some of them are, anyway." That was an even better position, one Lady Darriby-Jones certainly could not mount an argument against. "That Morgan is nice enough, pretty bright, too."

"Well, at least we have one proper police officer," Lady Darriby-Jones laughed. "Now, why don't you tell me about the difficulties you had with Mr Clambers, so that I can see what can be done about it."

"Shan't, won't, it's not right."

They were back at square one. Lady Darriby-Jones needed to try a different tack.

"Do you remember that humdinger of a row you had with Ali over her horses?"

"Yes, how could I ever forget how stupid she was towards me?"

"Well, as you know, there are two sides to every story, just as there are two sides to every coin. You think she was being silly, stupid, and unkind? She thought, well, she thought something else entirely."

"Anyway, I'm not into riding so much. It's all archery now. I'm the London West girls champion, you know? I'm now competing in the regionals hosted by the Barrows of Barrow Long. You know them, don't you?"

"Yes, very well, but you see, my point is that if you have one distinct point of view, then you can see that the police might have a different perception of it entirely."

"I'm still not telling you what we were fighting about." This was said with her chin jutting out into the world like the figurehead of a great ship of state.

It was clear that Lady Darriby-Jones wasn't going to extract any more information from Lucy Mason. She would have to be content with what she had already.

Which was not an awful lot. Or she could work around it in a different way.

"Lucy, what's so special about this archery tournament at the Barrow place?"

"What's so special? It's the biggest tournament in the south of England. I had to win the West London league just to get entered into this tournament. Oh, everyone is going to be there and..."

"You must stay with us, of course. No, Lucy, it's a must. The Barrows will be far too busy and Smith can take you over there each day it's on. We'd love to have you."

"Well, you sort of are anyway, aren't you?"

"I don't..." but then she did and smiled to show her appreciation of the joke. "Yes, the Darriby Dungeon is owned by us so really you're staying with us already. But, seriously, Lucy, when you get out of this place, I want to see you at Darriby Hall where you'll be most welcome."

Lady Darriby-Jones had an ulterior motive, of course. If she couldn't get Lucy to talk now, she would manage it during a long weekend with Lucy a guest at Darriby Hall.

. . .

That's when the plan fell apart for the simple reason that the door slammed. There was only one person she knew who could slam a door like that, as if the door was being shut on a life sentence.

If Manners knew that Lady Darriby-Jones was here talking to the person helping the police with their enquiries, his rage would know no limit. Maeve clearly had the same idea because she entered the tiny interview room at that precise moment, declaring that Lady Darriby-Jones must hide.

Of course, there was only one place to hide in the tiny police station.

"Quick," said Maeve, "follow me." She led the way back to the single cell the police station offered. "Under the bed," she said, "I'm sorry, Lady Darriby-Jones, but it's the only safe place to hide."

This proved quite a task for Lady Darriby-Jones, in which both Maeve and Lucy had to assist while the grumpy, demanding voice of Manners moved nearer and nearer. Ever since she had decided on the new uniforms for the staff at Darriby Hall, Millie, her maid, had selected the tightest skirts imaginable for Lady Darriby-Jones. Whether chasing fashion because Millie no longer looked the slightest bit fashionable in her smart but dreadfully full uniform, or out of a thirst for revenge, Lady Darriby-Jones didn't know.

But what she did know is the new skirts Millie had procured from somewhere were going to make it hard to get down under the bed.

And an awful lot harder to get back up again.

With two young and fit people, one on either side, she managed to make it down, just before Manners entered the cell area.

"What are you doing in here, Morgan?" he asked.

"I thought to try and question the suspect some more, didn't I, sir?" she replied fluidly, making Lady Darriby-Jones immensely proud of her fellow Cardiffian.

"Excellent. Did she admit anything?"

"No sir, not a sausage and that's because I don't think she's..."

"Just charge her anyway, sergeant. I can't be bothered with all this palaver. I'm going home in a moment. I only managed four holes and who did I see coming up behind me?"

"The commissioner, sir?"

"How did you know?"

"Oh, call it a hunch, sir, or perhaps it's just bad luck working its way through the system, sir."

Lady Darriby-Jones, lying immobile under the bed, considered Maeve's last comment to be particularly appropriate. If you make your own good luck through your attitude, it stands to reason that a poor attitude means you're bringing bad luck down on yourself.

Chapter Five

Lady Darriby-Jones made her escape from the Darriby Dungeon with the help of several police officers leveraging herself out and up from down in under the bed set up for whoever the prisoner happened to be. In this instance, it was Lucy Mason, although Lady Darriby-Jones had, too, experienced what it was like to have that door slam shut with her on the wrong side of it.

Manners had a lot to answer for, she ruminated as she made her way home once the chief inspector had departed a second time and Maeve had declared the 'all clear'. Millie, her maid, had some answering to do as well, with these daft skirts getting tighter and tighter in some mad rush of revenge for the new staff uniforms.

She went, first, to the library, in need of a pink gin, knowing that Torino would be hovering around somewhere close by, ready to pour at a moment's notice.

She was spot on. As she approached the library door, it opened from the inside and Torino stood there.

"How did...?"

"I heard the front door open and close again, milady, but no bell had rung. That meant it had to be a member of the family. Lady Alice always uses the side door and I didn't imagine his lordship would be here until much later and Mr Burrows, milady, is here in the library, so that only..."

"Left me, yes, well done, Torino. We'll make a detective of you yet."

"Oh no, milady, that might interrupt my duties and I'd never stand for that, milady."

"You always say just the right thing, as well, Torino. Can you manage three more right words?"

"Three more words, milady?" He was clearly puzzled, something that Lady Darriby-Jones rather enjoyed.

"Let me give you a clue, Torino. The first is a colour, a particularly feminine colour. The second is... well, that would give it away entirely and the third is just my name, or my title? Actually, I wonder which it is."

"Pink gin, milady?" Torino managed this with a completely straight face, despite the double enquiry contained within the phrase.

Did she want a pink gin and were these the right three words?

"Why, yes, that would be lovely. One for Mr Burrows too, please Torino. You know how he's partial to an occasional pink gin." She crossed over to where Alfie sat, noting how he politely stood as soon as he noticed a lady approaching him.

"Good evening, Lady Darriby-Jones," he said, reminding her that he would need to call her something else when he was married to Lady Alice, her daughter. Quite what, she had no idea at present.

"Good evening, my dear. Torino is bringing something to fortify you in your endeavours, but you must tell me what you're trying to do."

"I heard about the Darriby Myth, of course."

"Why," Lady Darriby-Jones replied, a little too breezily for comfort, "would that bring you here? Oh, I see, you want to delve into it. Well, that's no bad thing, I do believe. After all, we need to know whether it's based on fact or fiction, don't we? If only to help poor Lucy."

"Exactly, Lady Darriby-Jones. I must admit I've become fascinated by it. Ali told me all about it this afternoon and I've not been able to get it out of my mind."

"Well, dig and delve then, Alfie, my dear, for soon I'll need you on a real case, by which I mean a case going on right now. Ah, here's Torino."

After the drinks had been served, Lady Darriby-Jones sat beside Alfie and they went together through the various snippets of information that Alfie had located.

"There's not a lot here, Alfie," she said at two-thirds of their glasses left to go.

"Nothing much at all," he admitted when the middle third had disappeared.

"I think you need a bigger library," Lady Darriby-Jones

suggested when just a finger left. "Why don't you go to Oxford? There are scores of libraries in Oxford."

"I doubt they'd let me in," Alfie replied, reminding Lady Darriby-Jones of his working-class background; Alfie's father had been a coal delivery man. Alfie, himself, had received just a threadbare elementary education; after the age of fourteen, he was entirely self-taught.

In many ways not so different to Lady Darriby-Jones, Lady Alice, Darriby himself and a host of their friends and acquaintances. Putting all of them together, there had been a few schools, a host of governors and governesses of varying durations, and many gaps between in which there hadn't been much at all.

Lady Darriby-Jones rather liked the idea that she had been largely self-taught, although she felt conscious that her ignorance on many matters often showed, whereas Alfie seemed to have a knack for picking up knowledge.

Wealth hides quite a few cracks, but Alfie Burrows had grown up with a distinct lack of any form of monetary cushion.

"Oh, dear Alfie, with a letter from me you'll be dining at the head table with all the deans and professors. But do you think there might be something in Oxford, somewhere? I mean to tell us about the Darriby Archer."

"You know, Lady Darriby-Jones, an awful lot of these myths are debunked when somebody looks into them properly. I don't think, for instance, Robin Hood was much more than a common thief with a liking for a certain lady. He might have preyed on the rich, but then there wouldn't be much point in robbing the poor, would there?"

"No, I suppose not, except there are other types of wealth, Alfie. Think, for instance, of intelligence, warmth, compassion, kindness and – dare I say it – love."

"What did I hear?" came a voice across the library floor that they both knew exceedingly well. Lady Darriby-Jones looked up to see her daughter moving towards the table they sat at, several history books spread out on the top to indicate they were deep into research of some form.

"Ali... you, I mean, you..."

"Look lovely, my dear," Lady Darriby-Jones finished off for Alfie, who couldn't begin to find the words to describe how beautiful Lady Alice looked right then. Already changed for the evening, she had a mauve dress almost touching the floor, but sleeveless and strapless, seeming to stay on by willpower alone. Her hair, fashionably short since the autumn, was adorned with mauve and white feathers fastened to an orange headband. Around her neck she wore the famous Darriby Diamond, a rare purple one brought back from some campaign or other by Lady Alice's great-great-great-grandfather. Lady Darriby-Jones couldn't remember what number he was in the line of Darriby succession, but did recall that he had been a famous soldier, mortally wounded when fighting with Wellington in Spain.

Little did Brigadier Lord Darriby ever imagine that a hundred or more years after his death, a Darriby daughter would be wearing his diamond while planning her wedding at Darriby Hall.

"Aren't you going to change, Mummy?" Alice said, breaking into Lady Darriby-Jones' daydream.

"Is it time?"

"It's half past seven, Mummy. Torino won't be pleased if you're late. You know how he..."

It had happened again. Lady Alice didn't finish her sentence. Lady Darriby-Jones had noticed this more and more. As Lady Alice, once so fierce, feisty and biting with her tongue, had softened through a developing state of being, otherwise known as 'being madly in love', so her thoughts had become vaguer, as if they were made of the wind in the sails of a yacht, likely to dissipate one minute and blow a gale the next.

"But what were you looking at?" Once more, Lady Alice's changeable nature brought Lady Darriby-Jones back to earth. "Are you planning our honeymoon? Oh, do say you are! As long as it has horses, I don't..."

Again, she stopped, but this time she had picked up one of the books from the table:

The Rise and Fall of Everyday Life in Medieval Oxfordshire.

Written by someone with a number of letters after her name.

Lady Darriby-Jones wondered, for the briefest of moments, why one could have a 'number of letters' but not a 'letter of numbers'? Even an 'alphabet of numbers' would be acceptable.

"We're not going to Oxfordshire for our honeymoon, are we, dearest?"

"No... I..."

"I thought maybe South Africa or Argentina, someplace where there are lots of horses so we can ride every day, just you and me."

"We weren't planning honeymoon destinations, my dearest." Lady Darriby-Jones tried to calm the situation as well as she could. "We were looking into the Darriby Archer Myth."

"Oh, that old cobblers," she replied, "why on earth would you want to spend time with those smelly books? We've got so much to do now, Alfie, my dear. I want this to be a special wedding, one that people will never forget."

"I can do both," Alfie replied, a response which told Lady Darriby-Jones that he had it totally wrong.

"Both?" Lady Alice thundered.

"Can't I? I mean, it doesn't take long to skim through these books and determine what level of truth lies behind the Darriby Archer."

"It's not fair, Alfie, not fair at all."

"It will only take a day, two at most," Alfie continued, demonstrating again that he had a lot to learn about the distaff side, or 'managing the ladies' as some of their coarser acquaintances might put it.

"Mr Burrows..." This spelt trouble. When the name changed to the formal, it meant the man was really on sticky ground.

When on sticky ground, the best thing to do is get on a firmer footing immediately. Find solid ground, even if it meant retreating some distance, then build from there.

Unfortunately, Alfie did no such thing. He ploughed on deeper into the mire.

"It's important to me, Ali. Please understand that."

"All I understand is that you put some smelly books ahead of our happiness." With that said, she turned and left the library.

Lady Darriby-Jones remembered seeing a vision of loveliness moving away at pace, like a film reel put on the projector at too fast a speed.

Chapter Six

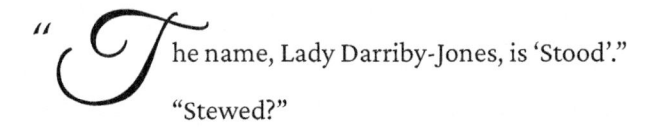

"The name, Lady Darriby-Jones, is 'Stood'."

"Stewed?"

The voice at the other end of the telephone gave out a sigh that spoke of having to explain the correct pronunciation many times a day.

"Almost, it's of Dutch origin."

Was that supposed to tell Lady Darriby-Jones anything? She had never been to Dutch, or whatever they called their country, but remembered a book from her childhood, with pictures of windmills interspersed amongst vast fields of tulips.

She loved tulips; they represented the best time of year, in her opinion, when the warmth of the sun really started to make a difference.

And the picture in her head of tulips is what made up her mind.

"Can you come down here, Miss Stewed?"

"No."

"You can't come?"

"No, that's not what I meant. I meant 'no' to the name. It's 'Stood'. Think of being misunderstood, but then change the 'o' to 'oo'."

"'o' to 'oo'?"

"Exactly, Lady Darriby-Jones. Now, ask me the question again."

Lady Darriby-Jones had to admit that she had forgotten the question with all the worry about pronunciation.

"You were about to ask whether Miss Stood was available to come down immediately." Miss Stood stressed the 'oo' in her own name, presumably following some pattern she had picked up in her school days about constantly reinforcing new learning. "The answer, of course, is 'yes'. I will get the next train."

"Excellent, Miss... eh... Stood, you go from Padd..."

"I know the route, Lady Darriby-Jones. I purchased tickets for both poor Mr Clambers and for the wicked Lady Mason. London Paddington to Oxford where one changes for Darriby Halt. I'll look up the timetable and telephone you back as soon as I know. Please meet me at the station."

Lady Darriby-Jones tried, twice, to tell Miss Ursula Stood that Smith would meet the train at Darriby Halt and bring her by car to Darriby Hall, but was told firmly that the murder of Mr Clambers put the wedding at incredible risk of being totally unplanned and, consequently, she must have Lady Darriby-Jones' complete attention throughout her visit, "from the very first moment to the very last".

"I don't have need of a rest after my journey," Ursula Stood said on arrival. "I will merely freshen up and meet you in a moment. In the meantime, you can be setting up an operational room."

"What?" Lady Darriby-Jones had heard of 'ops rooms' from the detective books she consumed by the dozen, but hardly thought they would apply to planning a wedding.

"We need a mid-sized room away from the hustle and bustle to be our central planning area," the tall, thin, middle-aged lady said as she wandered around the ground floor of Darriby Hall. "What's in here?"

"That's my private sitting room, Miss Stood," Lady Darriby-Jones replied, then the dreadful hand of fate appeared as she realised Miss Stood's intention.

"Excellent, far better a private room than a public one where everyone can come and go as they please. This is a little cramped but should suffice if we are careful. Now, what's that fellow called?"

"You mean Torino, our butler?"

"Yes, of course I do." She had a way of talking that made her always right; consequently, the person with whom she was conversing was always wrong. "Have Torino set the room up appropriately. We need to push the sofas and large chairs out of the way and have three tables or desks with dining chairs and a large filing cabinet. Additionally, I would much prefer a screen around my desk, although yours and Lady Alice's may be open to all if you prefer. I will need this ready immediately after my freshen up and tour of the main rooms and grounds. Is that possible, Lady Darriby-Jones?"

"Don't you want to know what we want for the wedding first?" she asked in reply, wondering what on earth she had plunged into in asking for backup to be sent from the firm of Clambers and Mason.

"I know exactly what you want, Lady Darriby-Jones. The question we need to address is how we will get it done by the time of the wedding."

Lady Darriby-Jones agreed; there seemed little point in arguing the position with Miss Stood.

"Of course, Miss Stood. Torino, did you hear what the lady needs?"

"Don't assume, Lady Darriby-Jones. Repeat the instructions to your butler. At least that way I can be sure you have understood them yourselves."

Lady Darriby-Jones resented the requisition of her private sitting room, her favoured sanctuary. But, if it meant getting the wedding organised, so be it. She didn't like it, but she would lump it, to alter an expression Lady Alice had used a lot in her childhood.

The problem didn't lie with the lack of use of her sitting room, but with another facet that she had completely overlooked.

Miss Ursula Stood, for all her brusqueness and appearance of efficiency, was completely disorganised.

She also knew best on every occasion, sighing constantly, as an actor might do on stage in a comedy play when driven to distraction by the incompetence of all those around her.

Within the first two hours of Miss Stood being in charge, they had changed the location of the marquee four or five times, altered the timetable on repeated occasions and turned the whole planning that Mr Clambers, Lady Darriby-Jones and Lady Alice had started, on its head.

"I don't know where we are and what's going on," Lady Alice said. To be fair, the relationship between Lady Alice and Miss Stood had gone rotten from the first. Lady Alice had been riding when Lady Darriby-Jones had gone in the Rolls to meet her train. Her daughter had ensured she was back in time for Miss Stood's arrival at Darriby Hall, but Miss Stood had immediately said that a riding dress was not appropriate for a bride-in-planning.

"I'll wear what I like in my own home," Lady Alice had said with a flash of her old fiery temperament that Lady Darriby-Jones welcomed this time around.

"I expect my clients to behave and dress appropriately..." Miss Stood started her reply, but it ran out of steam when Lady Alice turned her back on her and marched away.

"It is difficult, my dear, but you have to bear in mind that she is a professional and we are very much in need of her expertise if we are to get everything organised in such short order."

"I suppose so, Mummy, but I'm not happy about it."

Darriby had dealt with the situation as, on reflection, Lady Darriby-Jones had expected her husband to. He took one look at Miss Ursula Stood and turned away, walking back to his sluggery, calling over his shoulder that it was very nice to meet Miss Stewed, but he really had a lot on.

"The War Office is very interested in breeding poisonous slugs as a weapon. They believe they can be dropped by..." But he was, by that time, too distant for the group of wedding planners to hear what the War Office might do with a battalion of poisonous slugs.

"I like that, Daddy," Lady Alice called after him, "perhaps a regiment called 'The Royal Slugs' and you can be colonel-in-chief."

But Lady Darriby-Jones knew that Lady Alice detested the slugs every bit as much as she, herself, did. Lady Alice's fascination with the new army unit was because her father had taken a stance against Miss Stood, not from some latent respect for her father's work.

The afternoon wore on with repeated instances of confusion and mind changing. Lady Darriby-Jones joked about women always changing her mind and we had to live with it, but, she had to admit; she was as confused as anyone by the time they retired to dress for the evening.

Millie came up with the answer, and Lady Darriby-Jones blessed her for the idea.

"You do know what she's called below stairs, milady?" Millie said, after hearing a regular rant from Lady Darriby-Jones about the new wedding planner.

"No, tell me, Millie."

"I believe her first name is Ursula?"

"It is. What of it?"

"She's been named downstairs as 'Miss Understood'." Millie did a passable attempt at a Dutch stress to go halfway between the English of 'understood' and the Dutch 'stood'.

"Very good, Millie. She seems to spin misunderstanding with everything she touches."

"She's got below stairs fair exasperated, milady. I said to them, I did, why doesn't her ladyship take charge? She could do it easily and for far less cost than paying for expensive wedding planners just for the sake of it."

"What did the others say to that?" It had occurred to Lady Darriby-Jones, but she doubted she had the expertise.

"Oh, they were all for it, milady, saying it would be such fun to get ready for the wedding with just family... well, I mean, like, family and..."

"No, Millie, you're spot on. You're not to worry about overstepping the mark in talking to me. We are all a big family, or tribe, or whatever you want to call it. I like it that way and wouldn't have it any other way."

"Thank you, milady. Does that mean that you..."?

"Yes, I do believe I might. I'll need to talk to Lady Alice about it and may not send 'Miss Understood' back to London because it would hurt her feelings, but I quite like the challenge to do it all ourselves, keeping it in the family."

Chapter Seven

*S*urprises don't always come in threes, but they often come in a series and the next morning had two in quick succession.

Maeve Morgan turned up just after Lady Darriby-Jones had finished her breakfast, a meal in which she had contemplated Millie's suggestion and received an endorsement from Lady Alice.

"Yes, that would be super, Mummy. I'm sure you could do a much better job than Miss Understood." Her nickname had spread like wildfire; probably, Lady Darriby-Jones considered, because it suited her bumbling disguise of efficiency perfectly.

Lady Darriby-Jones was about to suggest that Maeve and she go to her private sitting room, when she remembered that the room had been commandeered by Miss Understood. They made do with the deserted billiard room instead, finding a bench under the window to sit on.

"It's about Lady Mason," Maeve started.

"Who?"

"Lucy Mason, the suspect the chief inspector pulled in."

"Ah, of course, for some reason she never uses her title, so I didn't recognise it."

"DCI Manners appears to be hell-bent on getting her up before a magistrate. He told me to charge her the other day; you probably heard that, Lady Darriby-Jones, as I believe you were hiding under the bed at the time!"

"The things we do for our 'profession'," Lady Darriby-Jones laughed, "but what type of trouble is she in?"

"He's determined to fit her to the crime, if you see what I mean, isn't he just?"

Lady Darriby-Jones did see what she meant. She had read in several detective novels of 'fitting' some poor innocent to a usually heinous crime. It was also a core part of Manners' modus operandi, as Alfie would call it.

"I managed to avoid charging her the other day, saying the evidence was incomplete and we needed to do more investigation work first. However, Mr Manners is going away for a week and is insistent on charging her, despite the scanty evidence. He said it's just too much of a coincidence for it not to be her, don't you know?"

"He's going away, you say?"

"Yes, he always takes a week off in Devon at this time of year. He's travelling down there on Friday afternoon, or so he says, talking about it all the time, so he does."

"Leaving you in charge?"

"Yes, at least I suspect so. That's the normal protocol, Lady Darriby-Jones, for a week or so away. The trouble is he doesn't trust me to let her go. That's my assessment of the situation, so it is."

"But you can't hold her this long anyway," Lady Darriby-Jones pointed out.

"We can, because she hasn't been arrested yet. She's 'helping us with our enquiries' at present."

"But she's being held against her will."

"No, far from it. She's choosing to stay in the Darriby Dungeon, isn't she just? She says the grub's fine, better than she could rustle up on a camp stove."

"But I offered for her to stay here. Our 'grub's pretty fine' too!"

"There seems to be an issue with staying here, Lady Darriby-Jones."

"Ah, does that have anything to do with Lady Alice?" It was starting to make sense to Lady Darriby-Jones. The antagonism between the two young ladies must be greater than she had imagined. Perhaps that fact had a connection to her argument with Mr Clambers; it was something to think about.

But right at that moment, Lady Darriby-Jones needed to resolve the problem brewing at the Darriby police station. If Manners got his way and Lucy was charged and dragged before a magistrate, there was every chance that the girl would be remanded in custody, given the serious nature of the crime.

"So, your boss is going away for a week to relax and walk the Devon coastline?"

"That's correct, Lady Darriby-Jones, is it not?"

"Then we have the answer. You delay until he's departed and then you, as the senior police officer present, release the 'suspect' without charge."

"That's just what I was thinking, Lady Darriby-Jones, but I need a favour from you to make it stick."

"You want me to telephone the police commissioner?"

"Got it in one, haven't you just?"

The second surprise of the morning came when the morning was almost over. Some might argue it was strictly the afternoon, but Lady Darriby-Jones considered the entire period before lunch to be morning, postponing the advent of afternoon until she and the family had eaten.

It came in the form of a taxi scrunching its way up the pebbled drive and swinging in an elaborate curve where the drive opened up to the huge, difficult to open front door.

The door was answered by a maid who was completely confused when it was explained that they were the wedding planners. Lady Darriby-Jones happened to be in the hallway at the time and asked for an explanation.

"Emma Peter," the lady said, "of Peter, Park and Place. This is Mr Peter Park."

"I don't understand."

"We've been commissioned to arrange a wedding for..." she looked at the clipboard she held in her hand, Lady Darriby-Jones noticing it had a pencil attached to it on a chain. "For a Lady Alice Darriby-Jones to a Mr Alfred Burrows. Priority level is urgent following the death, at hands unknown, of the previous wedding planners. That means an immediate start if we're to complete everything to what is an incredibly tight schedule."

"I didn't commission you," Lady Darriby-Jones replied, barely managing to get the words out, such was her confusion.

"Then, perhaps you'd be so kind as to escort us to Lady Darriby-Jones."

"But I am..." At that moment, the gong sounded for lunch.

"How quaint," said Peter Park, the first words he had uttered. "Perhaps we can use that to summon the guests at the wedding."

"You'd better come to lunch and we can sort this out while we eat," Lady Darriby-Jones replied.

"That would be a sensible plan of action, I believe," Emma Peter said. "It's been a long haul to get here and they say an army munches on its stomach."

It did seem to Lady Darriby-Jones at that moment that they had an army of wedding planners swarming over the place, all, no doubt, disagreeing violently with each other as to the best course of action.

. . .

Lunch presented an obstacle Lady Darriby-Jones hadn't quite foreseen. Both firms, Clambers and Mason on the one hand, and Peter, Park and Place on the other, claimed top slot when it came to the ranking of wedding planner firms. Miss Understood wasn't a partner by any means, but, on the basis of 'know thine enemy', Miss Peter and Mr Park knew her well.

Disliking her intensely with the feeling reciprocated. Hence, lunch, despite being delicious, topped off by cook's world-famous apple crumble, resembled more the Somme battlefield than a typical country house meal. No bullets, thank goodness, but barbed comments whizzed from trench to trench, exploding behind enemy lines frequently.

"I don't understand," said Miss Understood, "why this other firm is even being considered. Can you perhaps explain, Lady Darriby-Jones?"

"So, this is Lady Darriby-Jones?" Miss Peter replied, "couldn't you have let us know?"

"I tried, Miss Peter, but, sad to say, you somewhat spoke over me."

"Well, at times like this, somebody needs to take charge, especially with Miss Stood interfering constantly. Did you know that Lucy Mason, currently under arrest for murder...?"

This was too much for Lady Darriby-Jones. "She is not under arrest. I only spoke to the senior officer this morning." This was a slight exaggeration, because Maeve would only become the senior officer when Manners slopped off on Friday afternoon. "She is helping the police with their enquiries. As you may, or may not, be aware, the murder of poor Mr Clambers was carried out by way of a long bow. Lady Mason just happens to be a leading expert in such things, so it's natural that they should call on her at times like this."

"We heard she's being held at the police station," Peter Park said.

"Not held, but staying there to be close to everything. They have a bed there, you know, don't they just?" She could see the warning signs of stress rising, because, like Maeve, she reverted to her native Cardiff speech habits when under the strain imposed by others.

So much, she thought, for all Daddy's elocution lessons imposed on her. When the chips were down, her roots reappeared with quite alarming speed.

Lady Alice, remarkably, then suggested a truce. She had barely uttered a word all day because Alfie had gone off this morning, armed with a letter from Lady Darriby-Jones that introduced himself to various libraries in Oxford. He had reflected much on Lady Alice's opinions, yet wanting to do this research badly. Lady Darriby-Jones had suggested allowing a day to work on it and then reporting back to see where they were. Alice had reacted badly to this and told him to shove off and not to bother coming back.

Back in the old days, she would have had her mouth washed out with soap for indulging in such language, but then everything seemed better in the past.

"Mummy and I will decide, but we will decide quite alone," Lady Alice said with a firmness that even made Lady Darriby-Jones pay attention. "In the meantime, you are both to occupy different parts of the house and not meet at all. Is that understood?"

A ragged chorus came back, but just sufficient, in Lady Darriby-Jones' eyes, to legitimise proceedings.

They had a plan, a last minute one, but still a plan. Lady Darriby-Jones and Lady Alice would decide in a cocoon of peacefulness.

Chapter Eight

When Lady Darriby-Jones woke on Friday morning, the first thing she thought about was that Freddie was coming that day. His parents had gone back to India and had asked if he could continue treating Darriby Hall as his home from home.

Lady Darriby-Jones had agreed immediately, saying that Freddie was most welcome at any time, day or night, in a winter's blizzard or the hottest scorcher that August could send their way. She had gone on for quite some time until the countess had, smilingly, said she got the picture.

Lady Darriby-Jones would go to the station to meet him, of course. Hang the various wedding planners dreaming and scheming about one of the biggest weddings of the year; she would take the time off to go down to Darriby Halt and meet Freddie's train. She was sure that Cess would come along too.

. . .

But plans don't always work out the way they are supposed to; Lady Darriby-Jones had that message reinforced that Friday morning in cold, gloomy February, where only the snowdrops and crocuses dared show their heads above the parapet of the earth; even the daffodils would wait a week or so in the hope of a little stronger sun to beat down on their pretty yellow petals.

The first thing was an absence at breakfast. She had been emphatic in the drawing room the evening before that breakfast would no longer be served after eight in the morning; it wasn't fair on the staff, who would have a great deal of extra work in the coming months with a high society wedding to get ready for.

All the usual crowd came down in time. In fact, as was her practice, Lady Alice had come and gone by half-past six, scooting over to the stables to ride one of her beloved horses. That reminded Lady Darriby-Jones about something she meant to talk to her daughter about. The bill had come in for a dozen handmade side saddles, as Lady Alice seemed no longer interested in wearing jodhpurs and riding a conventional saddle. She had paid the bill, but felt that Alice should start paying her own way out of her considerable private funds.

It's just that there never seemed to be a time to talk about such matters, not with weddings to arrange and people being murdered left, right and centre. Well, perhaps that was an exaggeration, but sometimes it felt a little like that.

The guests started trickling in around 7.15am. Breakfast at Darriby Hall was never a very welcoming meal; people tended to fill their plates and turn to the task of shovelling in food without much of an idea of others being around. By contrast, the other meals at Darriby Hall tended to be more sociable affairs, with idle chat and intelligent conversation in broadly equal measure.

For the guest contingent, Miss Understood arrived first, then Miss Peter, leaving just Mr Park. Lady Darriby-Jones expected him along at any moment.

It's just that Mr Park didn't come along at any moment whatsoever. And Lady Darriby-Jones had a sickening feeling from five past eight. This feeling grew with every minute of absence.

"Perhaps he's ill" rotated with "Maybe he's not a breakfast person" and "Maybe he's decided to give up and go home", that latter suggestion coming from Miss Understood, of course, and based on wishful thinking. But Lady Darriby-Jones knew the truth, felt it in her bones.

"Darriby, dear," she shouted, coming right around to stand at his right ear, the better ear of the two.

"Yes dear? How are you...?"

"I need you to do something for me, Darriby."

"What's that, my dear?" One thing about being married to Darriby, he was a first-class gentleman. Provided he was a few hundred yards from the nearest slug, he was as attentive and loving as on the day of their marriage, perhaps even more so, because their love had been a long, slow fuse, but burning all the brighter for its slow build-up.

"There are no other men here, with Alfie away in Oxford.

Would you mind awfully going upstairs to check that Mr Park is alright. He's in the..."

"Blue room, milady," Torino interjected quietly, not wanting to embarrass his employer with her lack of knowledge concerning bedroom allocations. "Shall I accompany his lordship?"

"I think that might be..."

"Fiddlesticks," said Darriby, "I'm quite capable of going myself." He did and reported a few minutes later that the room was empty.

"Did it look slept in?"

"I don't know, my dear, just that the bedroom, the dressing room and the bathroom were all empty. I went into all three." Darriby would never make a detective; to make the grade would require him making a huge effort to up his powers of observation and Lady Darriby-Jones didn't think he had it in him.

"Thank you, Darriby, dear, that's most kind of you. I'll take it from here." She rose from the table and went immediately to the blue room.

The bed did appear to have been slept in, something which raised Lady Darriby-Jones' worry level greatly, because it meant he had stayed the night, hence hadn't been called back to the office or 'given up' as his rival declared. She feared what had happened. "But," she told herself, "there's only one way to find out."

Luckily, there were enough people still in the breakfast room to take in the update from Lady Darriby-Jones and decide on the next course of action, collectively. Soon after, a search party was organised by Lady Darriby-Jones, then a second and a third. She arranged it so that the breakfast room became the centre of operations. Family, staff and guests all spread out from there, allocated to one search party or another and all sent in different directions by Lady Darriby-Jones, the objective being to cover as much ground as possible.

And to do it quickly, for there was still a kernel of hope somewhere inside her.

She sent Cess and her mother, Mrs Robinson, to Darriby police station with instructions only to talk to Maeve, thus avoiding Manners altogether. She needn't have worried on this score because Maeve was already in charge in Manners' absence; apparently, he had taken off early to enjoy a gentle day's motoring down to the hotel in Devon. Maeve immediately called in all available policemen to aid in the hunt, telling Lady Darriby-Jones that she actually left Lucy Mason alone in the police station with the door to her cell open so she could, "hold the fort, as she said she was willing to do so, didn't she just?"

The hunt for Mr Park took everyone's attention but yielded no results. They combed the woods between the village and the hall, then combed them again. Lady Darriby-Jones was insistent that trees would play a part in the finding, hoping against hope that she was wrong and he would turn up at any moment declaring an interest in horses or slugs or waterways; anything except being pinned to a tree by an arrow through the heart.

It wasn't to be. But the organised search didn't discover the body either. It was a forgotten young man who alighted at Darriby Halt station late morning. Finding nobody to meet him, Freddie set off for the three-mile walk to Darriby Hall, thinking it would do him a power of good after sixteen hours of travel from Inverness station. It was cold, crisp and dry, the perfect day for scrunching through lingering frost on the grass beside the road, so he told Lady Darriby-Jones afterwards. He put up his duffel coat hood, found some gloves in the pocket of the coat and set out for his home from home.

He took the short cut that ran past the dowager house, liking the fact that it would take him by the sluggery, wondering whether he should stop off and spend an hour with Uncle Darriby, or zoom on to see Cess and Aunty Darriby.

"Not really much of a contest," he said out loud. "I've missed Cess so much. Hello, what's that?" He explained afterwards that something caught his eye in the garden of the dowager house, rented now to an elderly couple who had made a small pile in sugar importation and wanted to live their last years in some style.

But this something, while human, wasn't elderly at all. It had some youthfulness about it that struck Freddie, even from forty yards' distance.

It also had a lifelessness to it that sent Freddie's heart beating frantically. He had seen dead bodies before; you don't work as an apprentice to Lady Darriby-Jones without seeing the odd lifeless body from time to time.

But to discover one?

He leapt over the iron fence in such a hurry that he caught his school shorts and ripped a ragged tear in them. For one moment he was diverted into the explanation he would have to give matron when he got back to school after half term. Then, he was moving again, not caring about what matron would say.

"He was dead before I got there, Aunty," he explained to Lady Darriby-Jones when his cries had alerted the elderly couple and they had telephoned the hall, "but the body was still warm, despite the frigid air."

"What does that tell you?" Lady Darriby-Jones asked in reply.

"That the murder didn't happen all that long ago."

"Good work, Freddie," Lady Darriby-Jones said.

"Do you know who it is, Aunty?"

"Yes, it's someone staying with us. A Mr Park from the wedding planners..."

"Peter, Park and Place. Yes, I know all about them. I sent them here."

"You did, Freddie?"

"Yes, Aunty. You see, I got a telegram from Cess saying about Mr Clambers being murdered with an... oh, my goodness, it's the exact same method as Mr Park. Do you think someone doesn't want Ali and Mr Burrows to get married?"

"Excellent observation work, Freddie," Cess said, "but what have you done to your shorts?"

"Oh, that, just an occupational hazard, I suppose. It'll be a hot topic back at school when I tell everyone how I got them torn to shreds."

Matron still presented a problem, but the excitement of the moment far outweighed the prospect of explaining the shredded shorts.

Chapter Nine

"Oh, my goodness," Maeve said, the moment she arrived on site and could take in the scene before her.

"It's the exact same method as Mr Clambers," Lady Darriby-Jones said, mistaking the reason for Maeve's exclamation.

"No, it's not that. It's what I've just done, haven't I?"

"What have you just done, my dear?" Lady Darriby-Jones had a sinking feeling she knew what it was. She thought back to her encouragement of Maeve to do things as she felt fit when the boss was away. Had she just been imposing her own will on her friend instead of guiding her along a sensible path?

"I've only just let Miss Mason, I mean Lady Lucy out, or whatever her name is, haven't I just, Lady Darriby-Jones? Oh my, what a muddle, what a dreadful turn of events, is it not?"

Lady Darriby-Jones felt like tilting her head back and laughing out loud, only she didn't. Something about bellowing in laughter while a fellow human being stood pinned to a tree trunk, dead as a dead thing, struck her as inappropriate. Instead, she saw it as a lesson she could teach Maeve.

"When did you let Lucy out?" she asked her favourite police sergeant.

"Not twenty minutes ago. I could check in the log back at the station." She made to leave, to double back to the station to get the precise time.

"No, Maeve, think a moment; you're in charge now until Mr Manners gets back. What would your constables think if you hitch up your skirt and make a dash for it?"

"Yes, Lady Darriby-Jones, I get what you say, don't I just?" Obviously flustered, she wasn't doubling to the station but was doubling up on the questions at the end of each sentence. She then raised her voice, getting a grip, which was good.

"Bosworth, come here a moment," she called a constable over. Whether by luck or design, Bosworth happened to be the youngest and fittest-looking of the group.

"Yes, ma'am?" Bright too, to know that 'sarge' should be replaced with 'ma'am' as the senior officer on duty. Lady Darriby-Jones tucked that information away for future reference.

"I want you to double over to the station and check the exact time Lucy, eh, Mason, was officially released from custody. Also, because she hasn't been locked up all day, whether she is still in the police station. Then, if she is, ask her about her movements today. But do it innocently, not to make her suspicious. Do you see what I mean, constable?"

"Yes, Ma'am, straight away, Ma'am." He turned to leave, then thought of something else. "May I make a suggestion, Ma'am?"

"By all means, Bosworth, fire away."

"If this line of enquiry is going the way I think it's going, Ma'am, then it might be an idea to talk to Bates. You see, with his sprained ankle, he's been on desk duty all week and he and Lucy Mason got on like a house on fire. He would know whether she had taken herself off from the station at all."

"Good work, Bosworth, chop to it now. Let me see." She looked at the watch clipped to her tunic top, just like a nurse would wear on duty. "How long to get back there, question the lady, assuming she's there, and get back here?"

"Oh, I see, Ma'am, I'm to be timed, am I? Well, in for a penny, in for a pound. I'll go with fifteen."

"Right, top marks if you get back here and report to me by 11.30, black star if you're later. Got it? Any questions? Right, go, go, go!"

"Goodness me," said Lady Darriby-Jones when Bosworth had sprinted off towards the village, "that was first-class stuff Maeve, really spot on. Stay in the force and I predict you'll have Sir Peter's job as commissioner one of these days."

"Unfortunately, that's unlikely, Lady Darriby-Jones," Maeve replied, explaining that you couldn't remain in the force after marriage.

"Are you engaged to be married?"

"No, far from it, Lady Darriby-Jones, but I do want a large family, just like I come from at home. I'm twenty-three. I'd love to make inspector before I go on the marriage shelf and lose any chance of an eligible husband."

"Is that why you've stayed in uniform?" she asked.

"Yes, the detective branch is even more riddled with prejudice. As far as they're concerned, women are there to make the tea and do the typing. Now, what should I do next, Lady Darriby-Jones, now that Bosworth is breaking the four-minute mile to get the information I need?"

"Well, I think you know, deep down inside you, at any rate. But if I were in your shoes." She paused a minute, thinking that she had always wanted to be in a police officer's shoes. If the marriage to Darriby hadn't worked out, she probably would have joined up, just like Maeve did.

"Yes, Lady Darriby-Jones?"

"Ah, sorry, I was thinking, yes, if I was in your shoes, I would want to determine the likely time of death."

"Yes," she said, forgetting herself for a moment and punching the air with excitement, "I mean, that's exactly what I thought. You see, Lady Darriby-Jones, I am learning!"

"By?"

"By what?"

"By what method would you determine the likely time of death?"

"Oh, I see, by the stiffness of the body."

"Exactly, bearing in mind that it's pretty frigid out here so the body will cool down quicker than you think."

"Yes, of course. Well, do you want to come and see for yourself?"

"Maeve, I thought you would never ask."

Lady Darriby-Jones had read quite a lot about determining the time of death. She felt she knew enough to get by, although she did hint to Maeve that they call out the Forensics team based in Oxford. She sent another constable, drawn in from another village to help with the search for Mr Park that morning, to get to a telephone and call the Forensics team. Frustratingly, the sugar-importation couple had turned their backs on modern science and, while there was a line to the dowager house, no phone was connected.

The consensus was that Peter Park had come to the end of his life on earth at around eight to nine o'clock that morning. Bosworth turned back up at exactly 11.30, but took until 11.32 to catch his breath so he could speak to his boss coherently. By that time, she also knew from Bates, hobbling around the crime scene, but an expert at digging up clues in unlikely places, that Lucy Mason had not left the station all day, preferring to play backgammon with Bates than worry about her future.

Bosworth reported that Lucy Mason was in situ at the station and had been released officially at 11.53am. The log further reported that the call to alert them to come to the dowager house garden had only come in at 11.56.

"If you remember, Ma'am, we were searching the other side of the sluggery when Bates radioed in that a body had been found over here. You told him, apparently, to leave Miss Lucy in charge and for Bates to meet you here. See here, Ma'am, I copied out the key events. Between seven and eight, Miss Lucy was asleep in her bed in Darriby Dungeon. Then she cooked breakfast for everyone."

"Yes, she's a good cook," Maeve said. "Carry on, Bosworth."

"Yes, then she and Bates washed up. We were called out at nine fifteen for the search and have been out ever since."

"Well, there's your answer, Maeve," Lady Darriby-Jones said a few minutes later. "It seems as if Lucy Mason hasn't been alone in the police station at any time up until the last forty minutes or so. I think you can breathe a sigh of relief that you haven't let a murderer walk straight out of your police station."

It was time to move away from Maeve Morgan, now much more firmly established in control of the proceedings and move to the body discoverer. She located Freddie, next to Cess, looking bedraggled with his torn school shorts, his socks down at his ankles and his tie all skewed. For some reason, he had lost his duffel coat. Then she saw Cess wearing it. The kind young man had seen Cess also shivering in a uniform not suited for the coldest days of the year and had insisted on her having his coat.

Lady Darriby-Jones ought to have a word with Mrs Robinson about thick new coats, probably waterproof macs also, to give maximum protection.

"Freddie, Cess, my dears," she called across the clearing.

"Yes, Aunty?" two frigid voices came back.

"It's too cold. I'm going back to the house. I've seen enough, anyway. Will you please accompany me as there are some things I need to talk to you about?"

Freddie looked at Cess. Lady Darriby-Jones knew that Cess was the boss in their relationship. Both had wild streaks, but Cess had a lot more common sense and self-control. Cess looked back at Freddie and gave a little nod.

"Coming, Aunty," Freddie called, touching Cess on the sleeve. "Come on," he said, "I'm perished, not going to stay alive too much longer!"

On the way back, Lady Darriby-Jones told Freddie and Cess about the long-ago murder, carried out, according to Alfie, in the winter of 1067.

"It was done in exactly the same way," she said.

"As if someone today was copying the murder of long ago."

"Yes, Freddie, but who would do that? Also, here's the big question: will solving the murder of February 1067 help to solve the two murders of February 1927? Or is there no connection at all?"

"The way I would handle it, Aunty," Cess said after a few moments of thought, "is to set up two teams of detectives.

One, per normal, to look at the current day murders, the other to look at the historic one."

"Two rival teams? Yes, I like that. Do you think we have enough people?"

"Well, there's us three, Alfie, Ali and maybe Mrs Robinson would like to get involved?"

"No," said Freddie, "I doubt it. She's probably going to keep us at our desks all day long over half term, meaning we'll only be part-timers."

"There's a problem with that supposition, Freddie," Cess said, a smile on her face.

"Really?" Freddie asked, all hopeful.

"Well, you can hardly turn up in the school room looking like a ragamuffin, can you?"

"Ah, good point, except my case is at the station, complete with several sets of perfectly acceptable clothes. You see, I've learnt just how particular your mum is, Cess."

"Well," Lady Darriby-Jones cut across their conversation, "I like the idea of two teams of detectives. I'll give that some thought and will talk to Mrs Robinson about a little time off. It will probably depend on your half-term report, Freddie. Did you bring that with you?"

"Oh dear, I don't know. It might be in my case."

"Never mind about that. I can always put in a telephone call to the school." Lady Darriby-Jones was a bit of a hero at Freddie's school, having rescued Freddie's parents from a nasty kidnapping and solving the murder of the old headmaster; she could ask for Freddie's half-term report to be carried down by hand from the Highlands to Oxfordshire, and the school would rise to the challenge. "Now, you two, I suggest some hot chocolate in the kitchen after you've both changed out of your wet clothes."

"Wet and hopelessly torn in Freddie's case." Cess, as usual, had the last word.

Chapter Ten

It seemed all go that mid-February Friday. As soon as Lady Darriby-Jones got Freddie and Cess down to the kitchen, where it was always warm, she tried retreating to her private sitting room, but remembered at the last minute that Miss Understood had commandeered it for her planning purposes; quite how much planning was going on, Lady Darriby-Jones didn't know. The lady seemed to be in quite a state every time she ran into her, fussing over the paper for the invitations or the place name cards or the order of service. Weddings seemed to have become something to dread instead of a wonder to behold with two people coming together to share their lives.

On the way to the seldom-used upstairs sitting room in one corner of the house, Lady Darriby-Jones bumped into a figure hurrying down the main staircase, lugging her own suitcase as if servants had been outlawed.

"Miss Peter, I say, Miss Peter, what are you doing?"

"What, oh, it's you, Lady Darriby-Jones. I'm leaving. It's too dangerous here, don't you see? First one and then another. I don't know."

"Miss Peter, Emma, please calm down. You know, perhaps you need a stiff drink and..."

"Never touch the stuff, bad for your health, just like staying here is deadly. Poor Mr Park, poor Peter, what's to become of him? I don't know. Really, I don't."

Lady Darriby-Jones could, at that stage, have guided Miss Peter back to her bedroom, or even along to the upstairs sitting room with its glorious views across the hills and woods that made the outlying part of the estate. Once so situated, she could have reasoned with Miss Peter, attempting to calm her down. That would be her normal approach, but Lady Darriby-Jones really believed her too far gone, too wrapped in worry to be able to reason with her.

"Let me summon Smith to drive you to the station. Would you like a cup of tea or coffee while you wait?" No response, just a blankness; she supposed anyone would be so with their business partner pinned to a tree by an arrow through the heart.

Freddie had once calculated that with the volume of tea drunk at Darriby Hall each day, the water consumed exceeded that used in all the baths across both staff and family. She doubted he had the maths quite right, because it seemed you could put a lot of teacups into the bath and still get nowhere near filling it. She had heard about decimal places and imagined Freddie had got a few of them out of place.

Still, his slightly skew-whiff calculation was a useful way of expressing that every time something upsetting or eventful happened, a cup of tea came in handy.

As was the case right now. She had no choice but to fall back on her original idea.

Thus, through a mixture of comforting words and guiding with her arms, Lady Darriby-Jones managed to get Miss Peter up to the sitting room and placed into a deep armchair. She rung for a cup of tea, speaking down the tube that Alfie had rigged up one awful day when the rain wouldn't stop, then rung again to cancel it because Miss Peter had gone to sleep in her chair. Lady Darriby-Jones watched her for a moment, trying to work out what made her appear so strange.

"That's it," she said to herself, "the poor girl's so worked up she buttoned her jacket up all wrong." She was tempted to correct it but thought it better to let her sleep. She pulled a rug over the sleeping body and tiptoed out to the room.

And straight into Alfie.

"Hello, Lady Darriby-Jones," he said, reminding her, once more, that she couldn't go on having her soon-to-be son-in-law calling her 'Lady Darriby-Jones', but what would work in its place? Well, the wedding was still a few weeks off, perhaps longer, depending on whether Alice got her way or not, giving her time enough to ponder that one later.

"I was looking for you," he said. "You see, I wanted to update you on the research I've been doing into the original arrow murderer."

"Well, how many rooms do we have in this house, Alfie?"

"I don't know, Lady Darriby-Jones, maybe one hundred, maybe two."

"And can we find a room to be alone in?"

"Ah, well, there's always the east wing?"

"It will be freezing in there."

"There's an old paraffin heater in the green room. It's pretty smelly, but at least it's warm."

"How do you know about it?"

"Ali and I go there sometimes, just to be alone and to talk about the future."

"Well, we shall go there and talk about the past, won't we, Alfie? About eight-hundred years in the past, actually."

"Well, that's the thing, eh… um… Lady Darriby-Jones. I've been searching for several days now and not found a scrap about the original arrow murder, but I have found something else that seems quite extraordinary."

"Lead the way, Alfie. I want to hear this."

"I better go and see Ali first."

"She's not here, Alfie. When you went to Oxford to do more research, she kicked up a fuss and did her normal thing of riding off somewhere in a big huff."

"Gosh, we need to find her. Do the stable hands have any idea as to which direction she went in?"

"Alfie, she will be back, of that I'm sure. She's done this countless times. Good Lord, Alfie, you, yourself, have gone off on horseback with her before, not thinking to tell us where you're both going. You turn up a day or so later, as if nothing had happened."

"But Lady Darriby-Jones, I was with her then and am not now."

"I know, Alfie. I tell you what, if you like, just to put your mind at rest, I'll telephone the likely places she's holing up in and make some discreet enquiries."

"Yes, I would like that. Would you mind?"

"No, but bear in mind my enquiries will be discreet. I don't want her knowing we're seeking her as that will make the situation worse. I'll do it now, make the telephone calls, I mean, and we can meet later on in the green room to hear the results of your research. Is that a good idea?"

"Yes, thank you, Lady Darriby-Jones. That's a plan I can live with. But you will tell me the moment you find out anything, won't you?"

That meant diverting once more, this time to the study, where the single telephone was. Lady Darriby-Jones didn't know how he managed it, but Torino turned up at that very moment, hovering at the entrance to the study.

The telephone was his baby. If adoption papers were

possible for inanimate objects, Torino would have filled in the forms a long time ago.

"Yes, Torino?"

"I was just being here in case you needed anything, milady."

"Like the telephone, for instance?"

"Yes, or anything else, milady, anything at all." His dark eyes were, however, focused on the telephone. Lady Darriby-Jones knew the role she had to play.

"Torino, as you're here, perhaps you could dial me a few telephone numbers. We're running an incognito mission to determine the whereabouts of Lady Alice."

"Ah, milady, I'd be delighted to help. May I suggest you start with the Duxfords?"

"The Duxfords? Are you sure, Torino?"

"Yes, milady, I think Lady Alice and the Hon Steffi Duxford, their youngest daughter, are thick as thieves, so the expression goes, milady."

"Alright, we'll make a start with the Duxfords." She moved towards the telephone, but Torino covered the eight-yard width of the study before she could move across the eight feet gap she had to cover.

"Allow me, milady."

"Do you know, Torino, I do believe if you were bludgeoned to death you'd be pretty annoyed. Am I right?"

"Yes, I believe I would, milady."

"Unless the instrument used in the bludgeoning happened to be a telephone, then I believe you would depart this world a happy man."

"No, milady, I..."

"No? Really?"

"I mean, I'm not sure I could ever be happy separated from the Darriby-Jones family, milady."

"Ah, well said, Torino. Now, the first phone call."

They ended up making a wager on who was harbouring Lady Alice. They drew blanks with the Duxfords and the next two friends they called. Then Lady Darriby-Jones suggested a competition element to their task. "You select a name and then I do, then back to you. If I get it right, Torino, you'll wear your jacket backwards for a day."

"And if I select the right house, milady?"

"Then... um, I know, I'll serve you a pink gin in the library every day for a week."

They went through various selections, all without success, and were getting low on ideas of who to call next. Lady Darriby-Jones racked her brain, wanting to come up with the winning name to telephone, but none would come to mind.

Then there was a disturbance, a knock on the door. Torino had to leave his precious telephone and move back across the study to open it.

"Miss Stood, milady," Torino said.

"Ah, there you are, Lady Darriby-Jones. I've been meaning to ask you who Lady Alice's godfather is so we can make some special arrangements for him at the wedding."

Lady Darriby-Jones looked at Torino and Torino looked at Lady Darriby-Jones. They both said the name together:

"Lord Fork."

"Ali will have gone to Lord Fork's home, despite the fact that he's overseas somewhere," Lady Darriby-Jones confirmed and Torino followed up with a telephone call to the butler of Fork Castle, with a bewildered Miss Understood looking on.

Their competition ended as a draw, neither side winning. Lady Darriby-Jones felt rather relieved; she would not have wanted to lose, but, equally, would not want to see Torino ridiculed in front of his staff.

Dignity, she considered, was a valuable commodity, especially amongst those without the ready cash to ignore convention and do as they pleased.

Chapter Eleven

Lady Darriby-Jones felt the frigid air in the unheated east wing, that part of the house they had abandoned for the time being, containing, on the ground floor, the ballroom, several ornate reception rooms, the theatre and, of course, the much smaller green room attached to the stage in the theatre. That was her destination, but on the way, she admired, as she did every time she came through the east wing, the beautiful panelling and exquisite plasterwork. It was there to be admired, so long as you didn't stand below any vulnerable looking lumps of it.

It spoke of days gone by, when musicians and visiting acting tropes would have entertained large households and endless parties. Nowadays, they were limited to a few dozen house guests at a time; but Darriby, as a child, remembered the tail end of the old days when there had seemed to be an endless supply of money.

Money wasn't at all short now, it was just that everybody

wanted their share, especially the government, where it went on waste and vanity projects.

Lady Darriby-Jones sighed as she worked her way through to the green room, knowing that circumstances were in constant flux, changing all the time.

"We've just got to make the most of it," she said to herself, realising that phrase had become her mantra:

Make the most of it

She thought she did a damned fine job of making the most of it. She had a happy household. For whatever reason, Darriby Hall had been less welcoming when she had first arrived here as a new bride, some twenty-two years ago. She must have rubbed something of her character off onto the fabric of the building.

She gave herself credit where credit was due.

Those thoughts aside, she was glad when she arrived at the green room. She felt the heat of the paraffin heater before she saw Alfie, who had kindly dusted off an armchair for her to sit in.

"Well," she said, "where do we start?" She knew exactly where she ought to start, but wanted to tease Alfie just a little first.

"Have you news of Ali? Is she alright?"

"Oh, about Ali," she replied, but could not play the game any longer, not with a straight face. "Yes, she's fine, Alfie."

"Thank God for that. Where is she?"

"She's staying at Lord Fork's house, although Lord Fork is still in Papua New Guinea, or at least he should be on his way home soon if he's to make it in time for the wedding. Lord Fork's butler told Torino that Ali is treating the house as her own."

"That sounds like Ali," Alfie said, somewhat cheered, but clearly a little put out that Alice had taken off in this way.

"It's just how she is, Alfie," Lady Darriby-Jones reasoned. "It's how she copes with disappointment. However," she added with an uplift at the end of her words.

"Yes?"

"The butler informed Torino that she instructed for her horse to be saddled first thing in the morning."

"So, she should be back tomorrow?"

"Yes, that's what I think." Lady Darriby-Jones paused, then launched into a short speech she had been composing since bumping into Alfie that morning. "You know, Alfie, my daughter is full of faults, but there's one thing I'm clear about. Ali loves you to pieces, as, I think, you do in return."

"Yes, I know. Thank you, eh... Lady Darriby-Jones."

"We need to find another name for me soon enough, Alfie. We can't have my son-in-law calling me 'Lady Darriby-Jones', can we? Now, on to other matters. Tell me about your research."

"Well, there's something else first," he replied. "You didn't mention the second murder when we talked this morning."

"Golly, Alfie, you're absolutely right, I didn't. It went clear out of my mind. Strange to say, but that's the truth. I suppose with us talking about Ali, and your concerns about her, it just slipped into that grey area at the back of the head." She tapped the back of her head to add a visual representation, but the truth was she had no idea which part of the brain coped with different activities and wasn't much interested in finding out. "The murder this morning was of Mr Peter Park of Peter, Park and Place, the wedding planners. Young Freddie called the firm in from his school in Scotland and forgot to tell us he had done so. They turned up yesterday, causing a lot of confusion and some friction with the representative from Clambers and Mason, Miss Ursula Stood, christened by the Darriby staff as Miss Understood. Then, this morning, the exact same murder happened with Mr Park as with Mr Clambers. It almost seems like someone's got their guns blazing for wedding planners."

"The exact same, you say? Pinned by an arrow through the heart? Where was Lucy Mason at this time?"

"Funny you should ask that question because Maeve and I were just working that out, not half-an-hour ago. It couldn't have been Lucy because she was in police custody at the time, well, loosely at least. She was in the police station but free to come and go, although Manners wanted to throw the book at her and lock her up forever."

"So, you've ruled out Lucy Mason. That's interesting because Ali said the same thing, well, almost, despite the huge antagonism between them."

"What did she say?"

"This was after the first murder, of course, but she said Lucy was a rat of the first order, scheming, vile temper, etc. etc."

"I thought..."

"But she also said that there's no way Lucy was a murderer. She ruled that out completely and utterly." Alfie said these words with the emphasis he knew his intended would place on them if she had been telling the story herself.

"Which brings us back to the 1067 murder," Lady Darriby-Jones said. "Can that murder be linked with these today?"

"There's a connection, but I have absolutely no idea what it is, Lady Darriby-Jones," Alfie replied, forgetting his hesitation over names in his concentration. "We need to find those links and fast. The trouble is, I haven't yet been able to find anything to substantiate the story set in 1067. It's just not mentioned in any of the medieval chronicles, even the local Oxfordshire ones."

"Have you finished your research, Alfie?"

"No, there's more I can do, but I'm going to square things away with Ali before I go scooting off to the libraries in Oxford again."

"My bet is she'll be back here in the morning. Lord Fork's place is forty minutes by car, so maybe three hours on horseback."

"Good, I can't wait," Alfie said. And Lady Darriby-Jones knew he meant it.

. . .

But there was one other thing on Alfie's mind that afternoon. With the other points out of the way, he moved straight onto it.

"Inevitably," he started, "my research into the Darriby estate's past led to many different paths, all shooting off at tangents."

"The little oranges they serve in the hotels in London?"

"No, they're tangerines, Lady Darriby-Jones. I'm referring to tangents. Think of a line heading straight off from the edge of a circle. It's a mathematical expression, but in everyday use it means going off and away from the main subject, like the line going away from the circle."

"Ah, of course."

"It takes a lot of discipline to stay rigidly on track."

"I can imagine. So where did your research lead you, Alfie?"

"To a most curious discovery concerning a good friend of yours, a good friend of the Darriby family."

"Yes?"

"I can't be sure until I've done some more research, but it seems there's a connection between Morgan and Darriby."

"Morgan?" Lady Darriby-Jones couldn't think what Alfie was referring to.

"Maeve Morgan? Sergeant Morgan?"

"What? I mean what connection? Maeve's family comes from Cardiff, just a few streets from where I grew up. Her father is a coal miner. I can't imagine how she could be connected to Darriby."

"Well, this is where it gets interesting. Of course, I need to confirm it, but there could possibly be more as well. You see, oh, I really don't know where to start."

"Start at the beginning, my dear. That's generally the best place."

"Alright, well," he took a deep breath, almost as if he should be on the stage next door, preparing to deliver a Shakespearean speech to an attentive audience before him. "Lord Darriby had a grandfather..."

"Most people do, actually two, but go on."

"It is his maternal grandmother I'm interested in. Her maiden name was Grassby."

"Nothing like Morgan," Lady Darriby-Jones said, then thought her intervention rather pointless and vowed not to interrupt again.

"No, but her marriage to the then Lord Darriby wasn't the first time she went down the aisle. She first married a Russian prince, called Kostov. He died, I believe just before his thirtieth birthday, and they thought the marriage was without issue. It seems they were wrong in this matter, Lady Darriby-Jones. They had a daughter they called Catriona, or Katarina, something like that. Anyway, Marie Kostov, the mother, returned to England after her first husband's death, leaving her ten-year-old daughter with her Russian family. I thought it rather callous of her on first reading, but it seems Marie had little choice in the matter because the Russian side of the family blamed her for her husband's death and sent her away, keeping hold of the daughter."

"I'm following you so far, Alfie, although the blasted heater isn't giving off any heat anymore and it's like ice in here."

"It must be out of fuel. I can tell you the rest as we walk back to the main house. There isn't a lot more. You see, they weren't very nice to Catriona; that's the name she went by for her short life. She escaped from Russia at the age of twenty-two and came destitute to England in search of her mother. Unfortunately, Marie Darriby, as she then was, died in childbirth to your husband's father and the Darriby family thought this half-English, half-Russian an imposter and turned her away. To cut a long story short, she married a man from Cardiff."

"Mr Morgan, I presume?"

"Exactly, Evan Morgan, but poor Catriona also died when giving birth to Maeve's father. They had been moderately well off but fell down the social scale and Maeve's father took work as a miner, lacking any capital or any education, hence having limited options."

"So Darriby and Maeve are cousins?"

"Yes, distant cousins as I understand it, but there's one thing more..." he paused as he opened the door for Lady Darriby-Jones that went into the main part of the house. There they were met by a scream that pierced the whole house, coming, it seemed, from somewhere upstairs.

"Quick," said Lady Darriby-Jones, "we must see what on earth's going on now." They both headed for the main stairs, Alfie leaping up them, Lady Darriby-Jones being restricted to one step at a time by the dratted tight skirt that Millie had laid out for her that morning.

Chapter Twelve

*W*hile restricted as to physical movement, Lady Darriby-Jones had such an acute knowledge of her home, that she knew immediately from which room the scream had emanated. That, also, gave her an idea as to who had emitted the fearful cry.

She called Alfie back when he, quite naturally, made for the second-floor rooms, obviously thinking about Freddie and Cess, or perhaps even that Lady Alice had returned early from her visit to Lord Fork's place.

"No, Alfie," she puffed, "it's the main bedroom floor, the sitting room at the end."

"It's the wedding planner lady, then?"

But Lady Darriby-Jones had no more air in her lungs, all had been expelled on her race up the stairs. She nodded vigorously, hoping Alfie could see her action.

He did, but she now had a lead on him, so it was her that

swung the sitting room door open and gasped at the most extraordinary sight.

Two women facing each other across the room. She sensed, immediately, heightened tension. This was confirmed when her eyes took in more detail.

"Put the bow down, Lucy," she gasped, wondering how her voice worked when so out of breath.

"No, this little vixen murdered my business partner. She's going to go the same way." She stretched the bow, expertly bringing the feathered end of the arrow back to her mouth, squinting along the line of the arrow for her aim.

She had called Emma Peter a little vixen, but the target she pointed at was still big enough to ensure she could not miss, even if her eyes had been closed.

"Don't, Lucy." Lady Darriby-Jones moved further into the room, coming up behind Lucy.

"Stop right there, Lady Darriby-Jones, or I'll let loose the arrow right away."

That's when Lady Darriby-Jones made a decision. She took one look at the terrified bundle that was Emma Peter, still wrapped up in the rug she had placed on her earlier, and knew it to be the right thing to do. She stepped around a sofa and came out into the middle of the room.

"If you let off that arrow to hurt Miss Peter, you'll have to send it through me first, Lucy. No doubt you've got the strength to send it through the both of us."

"I don't want…"

"Then," Alfie came into the picture, "put the bow down, Lucy. There's no need for this at all."

"What? When she's killed two people already and tried to blame both on me? You can really say there's no need?"

"Alfie," Lady Darriby-Jones said, "go downstairs and telephone Maeve. Tell her to come here." She turned back to Lucy after noting Alfie doing as he had been told. "You get on well with Maeve, don't you, Lucy?"

"Yah, she's a brick, but she isn't the one in charge. I've got no time for that beast. Manners, his name is? More like Rude Manners."

"That's exactly what his nickname is," Lady Darriby-Jones said, "a thoroughly rude and bad-tempered man. Not remotely on my list of favourite people."

She had thought these comments to be a mistake, a further incitement to anger in a young girl already pushed past her limit. Yet, it seemed to work. Lucy looked across at Lady Darriby-Jones, smiled grimly. Then something caught her mind and she started laughing.

Still, the bow was tensed; the arrow aimed straight at Lady Darriby-Jones. There was still work to do in calming the situation, but Lady Darriby-Jones believed the backbone to the crisis broken, or the situation mended, whichever way one wanted to look at it.

Lady Darriby-Jones carried on with her reasonable reasoning, committing to the fact that she and Maeve Morgan both knew she wasn't involved in the murders, if for no other reason than the timing of the second one just didn't fit with Lucy's known movements.

"She could have an accomplice," Emma said, recovering in much the same way as Lucy was calming down, as if two sides of a set of scales, temporarily out of balance but soon to be back level.

"So could you," Lucy replied. "The only thing you've got on me is I happen to be an expert with a bow and arrow."

"And the fact that we were on the scene, ready to take the job over."

"But, Emma," Lady Darriby-Jones said, hearing footsteps on the staircase, "that doesn't quite stand up to scrutiny. I'm the one making decisions about the wedding, of course in consultation with Lady Alice and Mr Burrows. We didn't know about your arrival yesterday, until, well, until after you got here. It stands to reason that if we didn't know, then Lucy most certainly couldn't know, especially with her banged up in the Darriby Dungeon for the duration." She left out the bit about Lucy being free to roam, coming in and out of the police station and treating it rather as a hostel than a place of detention.

"I can confirm that," came Freddie's voice. Lady Darriby-Jones turned her head towards the door, seeing Freddie having changed into a pair of slacks, a checked shirt and a blue blazer, no tie, instead a cravat around an open neck. Behind him, white-faced, was Cess.

"Freddie found the body," Cess said with the authority of a doctor, although, strictly, she had another seven or eight years of study ahead of her to reach that status, "and the police have confirmed the death to be before 9am this morning. I saw the policeman who checked the log and he reported back to Sergeant Morgan…"

The Mystery of the Wettest Wedding Ever

"I like Maeve," Lucy cut through Cess' clinical rundown of the facts that would save Lucy's life, Emma's too, for that matter, "she and the others are alright, it's just that idiot in charge that's a problem."

"He's gone now, Lucy." Heads turned for another newcomer; this small stage was rapidly filling up, somewhat endangering the players, especially with a real bow and arrow a focal part of the scene.

But this latest arrival was the final addition, other than the return of Alfie, tracking along behind, his job of getting Maeve Morgan here completed successfully. Maeve stepped into the room and continued talking, her soothing Cardiff accent helping assuage all fears. "No, no, no, Lucy, my dear, this won't be solving anything, now, will it? Let's see if we can stop it right now and, perhaps, it can go no further, don't you think?"

"Yes," came a voice from an unexpected source, "I'd sooner forget about the whole thing and get out of here." Emma might have added 'in one piece' or 'alive and safe', but she actually didn't, having a head that was firmly screwed on and with all the connections now operating correctly.

That's when Lady Darriby-Jones crossed to the far side of the room and used the speaking tube Alfie had installed to request a tray of tea and biscuits with, "let me see now, six cups, if you could, Torino."

"Seven," called Alfie, "you must have forgotten yourself!"

All in all, as pink gin time loomed, a truce was arranged, washed down with tea and biscuits and appearing supremely successful, even to the extent of Lucy offering her hand to Emma and Emma grasping it warmly. Both issued apologies for jumping to conclusions about the other, just that Lucy's was more profuse.

After all, she had levelled a bow and arrow at Emma.

Lady Darriby-Jones understood that position. It's just that she didn't agree with it. Skulking around in backrooms wasn't her style.

Chapter Thirteen

*L*ady Darriby-Jones was back in the upstairs sitting room, the scene of 'The Near Miss', as Freddie and Cess were calling it. Emma Peter had been taken to the train station by Smith, strangely with Lucy Mason accompanying them in the back of the Rolls. Coming back from the brink of murderous intent, they seemed to have built a connection between them that threatened to develop into a friendship.

"I gave her my telephone number," Lucy reported back to Lady Darriby-Jones when she returned to Darriby Hall.

"You intend to see her again?"

"Yes, it makes sense, don't you think?"

"Actually, my dear, I don't see it, don't see it at all."

"Well, she had two partners until Mr Place retired. That left one, but Mr Park managed to get murdered, leaving her on her own. And..."

"And you, too, are on your own with the sad death of Mr Clambers. So, you're going to join forces, are you?"

"It's a possibility we might merge the two firms, Lady Darriby-Jones. How does 'Mason Peter' sound?"

"Very nice, Lucy. There's only one problem that I can foresee."

"Being?"

"The little I know of Miss Peter; she's going to want the name to be Peter Mason."

"Ah, well, we shall have to let you know on that one." Lucy had a shrill laugh, warm but rising in pitch as it went on, a little like an electric motor coming up to speed.

"We're meeting here," Lady Darriby-Jones said, "because, as you know, Miss Understood has taken over my private study. I want to tell you about an idea that Freddie and Cess had concerning the fact that we have three murders of similar execution and style, two in the Darriby grounds this week, one in the exact same grounds some eight hundred-and-sixty years ago. Over to you, Freddie."

"Righto," said Freddie, jumping to his feet, Cess following a second later. "The idea is simple. Two time periods means two teams. We split our resources down the middle, both go away and work on their different crimes, then we come back and compare notes etc. etc. Got it, everybody? Good, well, we've been working with Aunty Darriby to put together the two teams, so here goes." He paused, still in a state of indecision concerning who to put on which team.

The crux of the matter is that he wanted to work on the current murders, while Cess wanted to be involved with the historical one; but the obvious solution, to split the Freddie-Cess duo, had no appeal whatsoever.

"On the current team, we shall have Lady Darriby-Jones, Lady Alice, when she finally returns, Alfie and Smith, if that's alright with you, Aunty? On the..."

"That poses a problem." This didn't come from Lady Darriby-Jones concerning the allocation of duties to Smith, but from Alfie.

"What problem, Alfie?"

"I need to go back out to do some more research, not that I have much hope of finding anything, but there are some loose ends to tie up." He had promised Lady Darriby-Jones not to give specific details of his findings with regard to Maeve Morgan until he had confirmed and definite information. Hence, he was deliberately vague, not just as to the details, but where he was going to, too.

"If Mrs Robinson can be persuaded to assist, we can make do with the absence of Alfie, at least for a few days," Lady Darriby-Jones said, solving the problem within a sentence.

"Thank you, Aunty. Now, on the historical team, we're going to have Sergeant Morgan, Cess, Lucy and myself."

"I'd love to be a part of your team, Master Blythe," Maeve said, using his formal name because she was on duty, "but you may have to make allowances for me as I have other responsibilities, particularly while Mr Manners is away."

"That's fine, Sergeant Morgan," Freddie replied, secretly

relieved that it had all been set up without too many issues arising.

"There is one issue."

"Yes, Alfie?"

"Sergeant Morgan may be able to confirm or deny this, but I believe it's customary when setting up teams like these to give what's called 'terms of references'."

"Terms of...?"

"I see," Cess took over, "Freddie, it's just what we're trying to achieve with the team, what our objectives are, that sort of thing."

"Ahhh, well, that's easy. We have to find out who committed the murders." That seemed to go down a bit flat. Lady Darriby-Jones watched, ready to step in if Freddie made a hash of things, but praying he could sort something out.

That's when inspiration came to Freddie, raising the pitch of his voice by an octave,

"There will be a competition, however, to see who can get a 'result' first. There will be a special prize for the winning team. No, it's a surprise special prize, so I can't tell you that, now can I?"

When Lady Darriby-Jones left the upstairs sitting room, the others dispersing to their bedrooms to dress for the evening; she had another task to perform first, one that she didn't have much confidence in carrying out. After all, it was never easy to get anything from Mrs Robinson when education came into it, especially not with regards to her daughter.

"Mrs Robinson," she said after knocking on the door of her set of rooms next to the schoolroom and the old nursery.

"Ahhh, it's you, Lady Darriby-Jones. Just the person I needed to see, so you've saved me a hunt about the place."

"What can I do for you, Mrs Robinson?"

"No, you go first."

"No, Mrs Robinson, I insist you speak first of what's on your mind."

"Well, it's just that I thought Cess has looked a bit peaky these last few weeks. I know it's not the norm, but I was thinking of proposing a series of half days, mornings only in the classroom, so she has a chance of recovering. Then, when I saw Freddie this morning, it made my mind up and so, here I am, suggesting that they only have morning school for the whole of next week, the afternoons being entirely for themselves."

"If you're sure, Mrs Robinson? I mean, I think you know best in these matters."

"Yes, yes, we can tell them at the table tonight. Now, what is it that you came to see me about?"

"Ah, yes... eh, well... did you, eh, see the state of Freddie's school shorts?" She congratulated herself on coming up with a subject within seconds.

"Yes, dear me, boys and all that. I had to cut them up for dusters. They were totally beyond saving."

"Well, what will he wear for your classes, Mrs Robinson?"

"Oh, I've got some spares somewhere, Lady Darriby-Jones. Never worry about that. Smart bodies host smart minds, that's what I always say."

"Jolly good. I'll be off then, before Millie sends out a search party to recover my body."

"As long as it's not pinned to a tree by an arrow, Lady Darriby-Jones."

The following morning, Lady Darriby-Jones woke, got washed and dressed and made her way down to breakfast, very aware that the murders, even the one back in 1067, had all happened as they gathered in the morning to eat their breakfast. Well, she couldn't be sure that nine centuries earlier, they had a habit of eating at the same time as now, or even that they ate together, but in all other particulars, early morning seemed to be a dangerous time to be wandering around the Darriby estate alone.

That Saturday morning, however, everybody seemed to be present and correct. She counted them off on her fingers as they came, in dribs and drabs, down into the breakfast room and helped themselves to the feast of eggs, bacon, sausages, tomatoes and kippers that cook had prepared and the staff had wheeled in on trolleys covered in large silver domes.

Everybody present and correct. When Alice arrived later that morning, the full contingent would be there, safe and sound.

Alice, coming, riding through the woods, where the large oaks and yew trees were; the very type of tree that would look so impressive with a body pinned to it.

Alice's body, for everyone else had been accounted for.

"We need to send out a search party," she said, not quite believing that it might all be starting again.

"Why, what, who for?" echoed around the table.

"Lady Alice," she replied, her voice so quiet several people had to lean across the table to have any chance of hearing her.

"I've got a better idea," Alfie said. "If I leave now on horseback, I should be able to meet her en route. Let's assume she set off from Riversham at seven this morning. I think she will be close to Darriby village, on the Oxford Road, about nine o'clock." He looked at his watch, pushing his chair back at the same time. "That gives me around forty-five minutes to get to the stables, have a horse saddled and cover the three miles from the stables to the other side of Darriby village. I'm going to have to get a move on."

"I'll come with you," Cess said. "I just need to rush upstairs and put on some jodhpurs."

"No," said Mrs Robinson.

"No," said Lady Darriby-Jones.

"No," said Freddie, and,

"No," said Alfie, over his shoulder as he left through the French doors, onto the east terrace and jogging towards the stables.

. . .

It worked like a treat, as Lady Alice told everyone later that morning.

"My knight in shining armour was waiting for me. Well, actually, he was dressed in a three-piece suit, quite unsuitable for riding. But the important thing is he was there, waiting to escort and accompany me back home."

"Are you glad you came home, my dear?" Lady Darriby-Jones asked as soon as the two of them were alone.

"Oh yes, Mummy," she said, "and, like I said to Alfie, I'm sorry for going off in a huff. I don't know what it is, but I just see red sometimes."

This was alien to Lady Darriby-Jones, in the sense that she had never had a fiery temper; she could be like steel when those precious to her were threatened, but those flashes of anger had never been a part of her composition.

Thankfully.

Yet not alien, because she had brought up Ali, going through every conceivable aspect of her volatility. She still loved the socks off her daughter; in fact, she often thought she loved her even more because of her many and various faults.

Chapter Fourteen

The two teams of detectives had forty-eight hours of blissful working together, egged on by Freddie's urging of a mystery prize for the team that solved their mystery first. The 'present murder' team scoured the woods around both crime scenes, while the 'past murder' team tried to re-enact the killing of nine centuries ago, bickering mildly in their selection of which location was the most likely spot for murder.

Until, Alfie, about to leave to continue his research, made a casual comment about his recent reading that the woods around Darriby Hall had been planted by man, mainly during the reign of Henry VI, right when the Middle Ages started tipping into the modern era.

"So, Alfie," Cess said, "that means this would all have been open fields a few hundred years before, possibly barely a tree in sight."

"Exactly, it just goes to show that we can't use the current view of the world to govern our interpretation of the past;

things change over time." He looked at his watch, a very much cherished present from Lady Alice for his twenty-third birthday and turned to his intended. "I really do think I have to go now, my dearest, if I'm to make the train."

"Yes, you must go, my dear. Godspeed and come back to me the moment you can."

Lady Darriby-Jones heard this conversation of sweet goodbyes, wondering enormously at the change in her daughter.

Could love, such an unreliable and unpredictable emotion, really have produced such a change in her daughter? She would stay alert, of course; alert for signs of danger, but also out of curiosity that one Alfie Burrows could have come on the scene just a few short years ago and brought so much difference to the life of Lady Alice Darriby-Jones.

"I must insist on a word with you, Lady Darriby-Jones," the voice was thin, yet strong, reedy yet deep-set with something that also set her puzzling. She turned to face Miss Understood.

"Yes, Miss Under, eh, Miss Stood. What can I do for you?"

"I need your attention, Lady Darriby-Jones. Frankly, all this detecting business, while I'm sure it's fun, is detracting from the wedding planning. I must have your full and undivided attention."

"Oh dear, Miss Stood, I shall be with you directly." That had been her approach throughout the last few days; promise some close attention to the matter, but delay the start of it. The truth was she had started on a parallel set of wedding preparations, given the evident muddled incompetence that Miss Understood brought to the scene, but lacked the courage, or the brutal honesty, to sack this out of place character.

When Lady Alice had returned to Darriby Hall, all sweetness and light following the huff that took her cantering off to Lord Fork's place, she had endorsed her mother's approach entirely, entering enthusiastically into their own set of wedding arrangements.

And making pretty good progress.

"We don't even have clarity over the bridesmaids," Miss Understood complained.

"But you are making headway with the guest list?" Lady Darriby-Jones asked in reply. "We had decided that to be the priority, had we not? And Mrs Williams, the dressmaker, who did the new uniforms for the staff so splendidly, is, I'm told, striding ahead with Lady Alice's dress."

"Well, if that's the case, I haven't seen even the preliminary designs, Lady Darriby-Jones. I must insist on..."

"Yes, of course, Miss Stood, just not this very minute. Come and see me after lunch. You see, I have some pressing estate matters to attend to that cannot wait. Such is the life of the busy landowner these days. Nothing will wait..." she had moved steadily away while talking, pretending interest in some minor matter that the estate secretary would normally not even bother her with, something to do with repairs to the rose garden wall.

She had not mentioned to Miss Understood that after lunch she would be otherwise engaged because the team of 'murder past' had planned a massive re-enactment of the murder of nine centuries ago.

And, despite leading the 'murder present' team, she had every intention of being a part of it.

Lucy Mason was in charge of the re-enactment and she did an astoundingly good job of it, in Lady Darriby-Jones' opinion. She started with an analysis in front of both teams, looking at the position the dead bodies had been found in for the two recent killings, as well as various other factors.

"Ladies and gentlemen," she said, "you will see from Sergeant Morgan's photographs of the scenes that the arrow penetrated through the body of each victim and on into the tree. In the case of poor Mr Clambers, it went three inches into the tree, while with Mr Park it went four inches, possibly because Mr Park was of slighter build than Mr Clambers."

"Therefore, more of the power unleashed with the arrow was still around to penetrate the tree," Cess added by way of explanation.

"Thank you, Cess. That's exactly my point. Can you extend that line of thinking to its conclusion?"

Lady Darriby-Jones was impressed with the approach of both Lucy and Cess, looking at it as a scientist would, rather than as a member of the public.

"Yes, Miss Mason, the obvious conclusion is that the two

arrows were unleashed by the same person, because they seemed to have the same muscle power behind each shot."

"Exactly, assuming other points are consistent. For instance, the distance over which the arrow travelled."

"Yes, of course, Miss Mason." Lady Darriby-Jones had the feeling that Cess was a little disappointed not to have thought of that point herself. Still, she thought, that's the way young people learn and Cess would be unlikely to make the same mistake again.

"Now, let's translate that to the next stage of our reasoning. The story, as I heard it, is that the arrow in 1067 was lodged more than six inches into the tree. Now, I've done some practice shots over the last few days, not with a live body, I hasten to add, but with a sack of potatoes I pinched from the kitchens. My shots all lodged between two and four inches into the tree after going through the sack. Bear in mind, of course, that modern bows have more power than the old ones. That leads me to the conclusion that the murderer all those centuries ago had considerably stronger muscle power than I have."

"In other words," Cess added, "our long-ago murderer was probably a man."

"Most murderers are men," Maeve said, not as a dampener to their deductions, but to move the analysis on further.

"Yes," Lucy agreed, "but following the inverse of this deduction, with the more powerful bows today, it is perfectly possible that the recent shootings were carried out by a female."

"Interesting," Lady Darriby-Jones said, having held back from the conversation so far, listening intently and clearly in contemplative mood. "The question remains, however, why would someone pick on two wedding planners, usually people who bring joy and happiness into people's lives. It makes for fascinating analysis; I had rather assumed that to go through a body and still have the power to pin that body securely to the tree, it had to be a man with murder in their hearts. But this opens things up quite a lot. Now, as to the distance…"

The distance was important, incredibly so as it turned out. Lucy and Cess held the group spellbound while they worked out the probable location of the archer, using their estimate of distance and the recorded angle of entry. The first killing, that of Mr Clambers, led to a holly bush fifty yards back towards the house. Maeve confirmed that they had searched the area and found nothing.

With the second killing of Mr Park, found by Freddie in the grounds of the dowager house, there was a more complicated picture because of the wall around the gardens.

"I think," Cess said after pacing the ground a few times, "that the shooter probably perched themselves on the top of the wall right here."

"Isn't it too high for the angle of entry?" Lady Alice asked.

"No, not in this part where the wall has broken down a bit," Maeve replied. "This could be just the spot. What do you two think?" She addressed Lucy and Cess, both of whom had established themselves as experts in record time that afternoon.

"Yes, I think that's spot on," Cess said. Lucy took a few more moments, then confirmed Cess' conclusion.

Lady Darriby-Jones then made the next contribution. She tried to pace the yards from the wall to the point of death against the tree, but her skirt wouldn't let her get near to a yard a stride. "Freddie, do me the honours, if you will. I need the distance from the wall to the tree."

"Coming right up," Freddie bounded into place, "think of me as an arrow whizzing through the air." He started counting and came to twenty-eight before he bumped into the tree where he had discovered the body of Mr Park a few days before.

"Much closer than we thought," Lady Darriby-Jones said. "Maeve, do you think your boys searched this area when the body was discovered? My bet is that they concentrated on a greater distance away. I recall several policemen milling about by the rhododendrons, but none checking the ground beneath the wall."

"No, Lady Darriby-Jones, I do think you're right. It was an oversight."

"Understandable, because the general thinking at the time was a shot from some distance. But we should search now, don't you think?"

"Yes, but let's do it scientifically. She pulled some string from her tunic pocket and asked Freddie to get some stakes from the twigs lying around."

"How many, Sergeant Morgan?"

"Six should do. Whatever one calls a six-sided shape."

"That's a hexagon," Cess said, getting her answer in while Freddie was still scratching his head.

"Too right, Cess," he added warmly, "you're a walking encyclopaedia whereas my mind's a garden sieve."

"Not true, Freddie," Lady Darriby-Jones was quick to correct him. "Every brain works in different ways; hence people are good at different things."

With the string surrounding a wide area, secured with Freddie's stick-stakes, Maeve took charge, recalling her training about how to search a piece of land.

"First," she said, "we take a general overview, asking ourselves whether anything looks different or out of place."

"Yes," said Mrs Robinson, who had been quiet so far during this extended exercise. "The fallen stones look odd, almost like they've been moved into place."

"Yes, Mummy," squealed Cess, forgetting the protocol of calling her governess 'Mrs Robinson' in front of others, "they form a set of steps, don't you see, everybody?"

"And a firing platform at the top," added Freddie, equally excited. "Hey, you lot, we're onto something here or I'll eat my hat."

"You're not wearing a hat, Freddie," Lady Alice said, with just a hint of her old impatience.

"Alright, I'll eat my duffel coat hood. How does that sound?"

But the real discovery was still to come. As Maeve moved them on to the detailed phase of the search, Freddie and Cess lunged forward with enthusiasm. Lady Darriby-Jones thought it only right that they found the footprint at the bottom of the makeshift steps on the broken wall.

"It's massive," Maeve said, "must belong to a large and powerful man. Freddie, do you mind running to the police station and ask Bosworth to bring the plaster of Paris kit?"

"Not at all, Sergeant Morgan. So, you're going to make a cast of it?"

She replied that she was, but Freddie didn't hear. Having posed the question, he then shot away, heading for the police station.

That's the most that Lady Darriby-Jones witnessed that cold morning, because another movement in the bushes told her someone else was approaching. Not knowing who it might be, the killer maybe, or perhaps Manners come back early, she challenged the individual, asking them to come out into the open and let herself be known.

'Herself', because the movement she had seen was definitely that of a female.

Chapter Fifteen

The figure did reveal herself, coming out from behind the bushes and showing herself to be Miss Understood.

"Ah, there you are, Lady Darriby-Jones. I've been searching all over for you."

"Why me, Miss Stood?"

"We had an agreement, remember? We were to get together after lunch? The order of service, the number of bridesmaids, the speeches etc. etc. etc."

"Yes, of course. I was just finishing up here and then coming to you, Miss Stood."

"Well, there's not any time to spare. At least Miss Peter is no longer with us to stick her oar in, disrupting everything."

"I ended up rather liking Miss Peter."

"Oh, she's typical of the modern brand of wedding

planners, thinking everything can be done at the last minute with a wave of the wand."

"That would be nice, Miss Stood."

"That would be awful, Lady Darriby-Jones, doing away with all the careful preparations. Now, as we walk back, might I ask you about your detective findings-out? You know your reputation proceeds you, Lady Darriby-Jones, and I certainly follow your accomplishments avidly."

Something about her sudden switch of tone, from disgruntled school mistress to biggest fan, made Lady Darriby-Jones hesitate from divulging their latest findings to Miss Understood.

"Oh, nothing much," she said in a loud voice, hoping her fellow detectives picked up on her cautious approach, "just the usual frustrations, going up blind alleys and the like. Now, I know exactly what Lady Alice wants for her bridesmaids to wear..."

The extraordinary thing about the shoe print that Maeve had taken a plaster cast of, was the size of it, plus it looked very like a woman's boot, rather than belonging to a man.

"It narrows it down quite a bit," Maeve said when she showed the cast to Lady Darriby-Jones.

"Yes, but we can't do a Cinderella-type exercise of trying it on all the damsels in Oxfordshire for a fit," Lady Darriby-Jones joked, "although it is an excellent find."

She saw it more as a confirmer when they had a suspect, if they ever did.

The Mystery of the Wettest Wedding Ever

"Incidentally," Maeve added, "Lucy Mason has tiny feet, some of the smallest I've ever seen. I think she buys children's shoes to cope, does she not?"

"You like her, don't you, Maeve?"

"I do, not that the likes of me can ever mix in such circles."

"Well, you never know, Maeve, you held your own with the police commissioner and I count you as a dear friend." Lady Darriby-Jones thought of Alfie's revelations in the east wing; there had been something else Alfie had wanted to tell her about the Morgan family, something that the cries from the upstairs sitting room had put paid to.

"As do I, do I not?" Maeve replied, the warmest smile on her face as she confirmed her friendship with Lady Darriby-Jones.

Saturday rolled around without an awful lot of progress on the arrow murders, whether past or present, other than the cast of a single boot. That particular Saturday, the third in February and the day before Freddie had to return to boarding school, the weather warmed considerably, but at the expense of the heavens opening, sending huge sheets of water down to earth.

Or at least to their particular corner of northeast Oxfordshire.

"Well, any undetected clues will be well and truly washed away now," commented Freddie gloomily. In an ideal world, the crimes would be neatly solved within the half term holiday, so that he could entertain 'the lads' back at school with tales of mad chases across the English countryside.

The only thing that broke the weather-enforced stay-indoors domestic situation that morning was the telephone ringing at 11.15. And the telephone going off couldn't be immediately suspected of breaking the dullness of a dreary day with jigsaw puzzles and books pulled off the library shelves.

"Milady," Torino started, "the vicar of Darriby is on the line. I must say, milady, he sounds somewhat upset."

"What line?" Lady Darriby-Jones asked, clearly not yet fully conversant with the lingo of modern telecommunications.

"The telephone, milady."

"It's a line, is it?"

"The line, milady, goes from one apparatus to the other."

"Through the exchange," Freddie added, "that's like a great big connection centre where a bunch of girls link all the people together. You may remember, Aunty, you opened the Broad Stourton Exchange just after we had the telephone installed."

Lady Darriby-Jones had no recollection, but was sure Freddie was probably right. She went from the morning room to the study to take the call, closely followed by Freddie and Cess. Torino handed her the telephone and stood to one side, clearly not intending to miss out on the discussion.

"Vicar, how are you?"

"I've been better, Lady Darriby-Jones."

"Why is that, my dear man?"

"I have a whole load of guests in the church this morning, all asking after you and the bride."

"What do you mean?"

"They've come to the wedding, Lady Darriby-Jones. I tried to tell them it's a mistake, but they showed me their invitations and it's definitely today's date."

"But that can't be," Lady Darriby-Jones said. "The wedding's not for some time yet."

"Well, they've got invitations, Lady Darriby-Jones. I've seen them with my own eyes."

"How many?"

"Three pews' worth, but heavily skewed to the Darriby side. What shall I do with them?"

"Just a minute, Vicar. Let me think a moment." She handed the telephone back to Torino and asked Freddie and Cess what was best to do.

"We could go over there and explain," Cess said, "although they will be disappointed. How could they have come on the wrong date? I thought the invitations hadn't even been sent out yet."

"They shouldn't have been, but something's clearly gone wrong, very wrong." Lady Darriby-Jones looked at her two young charges. The same thought came to them all at that moment:

"Miss Understood," all three said.

But it was Freddie who added the idea that saved the day.

"Make something of it, Aunty, that's what I say. Invite them over here and make a fuss of them."

"But on what pretext?"

"Are, well, let me think..."

"I know," said Cess, warming to Freddie's creativity, "we can say it's a pre-wedding celebration, an assembly of all those near and dear to Ali and Alfie."

"Yes," Lady Darriby-Jones said, warming to the idea, "yes, we can do exactly that. Torino, the telephone please, if you would."

Twenty minutes later, a fleet of motor cars moved up the drive and came to a halt on the big gravel sweep before the house. It had been twenty minutes of hectic and panicked activity as everyone had rushed around to create a party out of nothing. Maids and footmen darted here and there, Lady Darriby-Jones noting Torino in his element as he created order out of chaos, thinking of a hundred things at once. He sent someone to the sluggery to fetch Lord Darriby, who came reluctantly at first but warmed to the task when he saw so many of his old friends.

Torino even remembered to arrange a collection of staff with umbrellas under which the three-dozen guests were whisked into the house, Lady Darriby-Jones, plus husband, greeting them at the steps to the front door, Millie holding an umbrella with a wobbly arm in an attempt to keep her a little bit dry as she stood to greet everyone.

It all seemed to be going exceedingly well until the last guest came up the steps, speaking crossly to the poor footman trying to protect him from the worst of the weather. The footman slipped in his haste to hold the umbrella over the guest, who cursed him as a particularly intense burst of rain came down on his shoulders.

That was when Lady Darriby-Jones looked up to see DCI Manners; who had ever thought to invite him?

The answer, of course, was Miss Understood. Nowhere to be seen right now, as is the usual situation when originators of chaos are sought for. Lady Alice eventually remembered that she had asked for a pony and trap to tour the estate in, having no idea of the disorder she had created in her wake.

Somehow, while not yet approving the invitations, she had managed to send out a batch containing a date and time that were hopelessly wrong.

"Mr Manners, how, eh, nice to see you."

"Well, you invited me," he replied, "unless you think I'm gate-crashing?"

"Gate...?"

"It doesn't matter, Lady Darriby. The important thing is you invited me and I'm here." He put out his hand and Lady Darriby-Jones shook it, steeling herself because she really didn't like the man at all.

"Manners, isn't it?" Darriby said, stepping between Manners and his wife.

"DCI Mann..."

"Security duties, I suppose?"

"Actually, I'm a-"

"Jolly good to see the police taking an interest. Just mill about a bit, Manners. I don't think there will be any trouble, but you never know. Got your truncheon with you? No, well, hopefully you won't need it, anyway."

Manners moved on into the building, glaring fiercely. Lady Darriby-Jones put her hands around Darriby's arm and squeezed it tightly.

"I love you, my darling man," she whispered in his ear.

"What was that, dear?"

"I love you," she knew she had to say it far louder if she wanted her husband to have any chance to hear it. "I said I love you, dearest", came out the third time, almost at the top of her vocal capability.

Several people turned to see the source of the overloud voice at the top of the steps. Not Manners, however, because Lady Darriby-Jones noticed him making a beeline for Maeve Morgan, making for another dangerous situation she would have to keep an eye on. Thankfully, Lady Alice came up to introduce her godmother, the dowager countess of Baritone and Strathfulton, the mother of Lord Baritone, the man who had been hanged at the tail end of last year for murder and kidnap, another case solved by Lady Darriby-Jones.

Thankfully or not, the dowager countess seemed totally unaware of the disgrace that hung over her family. Some wouldn't have invited her to a family wedding like this, but Lady Darriby-Jones never saw the need to blame a wider family for the sins of one member. Lord Baritone had turned out to be a thoroughly cruel man, but she would never put that cross upon his elderly and rather infirm mother.

Lady Darriby-Jones made a point to watch Manners carefully throughout lunch, and just as well that she did. He couldn't do much damage to Maeve in a crowd of people, but he was clearly watching for an opportunity to get Maeve away from the security offered by numbers.

That happened just as they left the dining room after a magnificent lunch that cook and her team had put together at incredibly short notice. The rain had paused and Maeve, declared to be a guest, as opposed to a police officer on duty, wore a beautiful dress borrowed from Lady Alice. She declared a need for some fresh air with no other than Lucy Mason, the two of them having rapidly become good friends.

But there was nobody in the whole wide world more designed to infuriate Manners at that moment than the figure of Lucy Mason, archer extraordinaire.

"Just a minute, Morgan," Manners said, clearly a little too much, rather good, red wine inside him, "what do you think you're doing entertaining a prisoner?"

"Sir," she turned around, her borrowed skirt twirling with the motion, "first, I'm off duty, as are you. Second, Lady Mason is no prisoner and certainly no suspect. You left me in charge and I made the decision to release her. She's actually been a great help in the case."

"Whatever do you mean, Morgan?" This, to Lady Darriby-Jones, sounded immensely menacing; she would have to act.

"I mean, sir, that she has provided huge technical input into the case, being an expert in all things bow and arrow and a highly experienced archer. I think you should thank her for her input... sir." That last word almost as an afterthought.

"How dare you, Manners?" Lady Darriby-Jones, moving in as swiftly as her tight skirt would allow her, wondered briefly why Maeve was making such a stand against him; did she know something that the rest of the world did not?

Whatever, Maeve was right in her decision that it was time to make a stand. She pushed through a scattering of people to reach her friend.

"Sir," she addressed Manners, "if you can't speak without civility, might I suggest that you don't talk at all?"

"I'll blast my staff whenever and wherever I choose," Manners replied, although he stumbled over quite a few of his words. "This one is suspended from duty with immediate effect, pending an enquiry into her disgraceful conduct."

Lady Darriby-Jones was certain Manners would have gone on to arrest both Maeve and Lucy on the spot, had he not suddenly toppled over and passed out as he hit the ground.

Chapter Sixteen

The 'pre-wedding party' as Freddie termed it had been a great success by anyone's standards, except, perhaps, that of Manners who spent the second half of the party snoring loudly on a sofa, before being driven away home by one of his constables, summoned by Maeve.

Whatever his drunken state, however, Maeve reported the next day that she had been turned away at the police station by a very sympathetic Bosworth, rather embarrassed at his promotion to acting sergeant.

"Did anyone tell you what the grounds for your suspension from duty is?"

"Yes, Bosworth gave me a rambling letter from Mr Manners. It seems I made a gross usurpation of authority in releasing Lucy, did I not?"

Lady Darriby-Jones thought she actually had not, instead following common sense, of which Manners had a yawning gap. She promised to call Sir Peter, the police commissioner, only to be told by his housekeeper that he and Lady

Duxford were away in South Africa and not expected back for three more weeks.

"After which, although I shouldn't really be saying this, Lady Darriby-Jones, but I'm sure he would want you to know, Sir Peter is retiring from his role."

"I had expected it, just not quite so soon," Lady Darriby-Jones had replied.

"Well, Lady Darriby-Jones, Sir Peter has very kindly left a list of who else to contact during his absence. You are in Darriby, of course. Now just let me see... yes, it says to contact Detective Chief Inspector Rory Manners. Do you know that gentleman?"

"Yes," she replied, "thank you so much for passing on the name."

Miss Understood was another one behaving rather badly at that moment. Lady Darriby-Jones reflected on this when Miss Understood returned late on Saturday afternoon, just as the guests were getting into their cars, thanking the Darribies profusely for a delightful 'pre-wedding party', several saying it was an honour to be included on the list of special people in the lives of the happy couple to be, one saying they would plan something similar for their daughter's upcoming wedding later in the year.

"Well," said Miss Understood on coming into the drawing room after the last guest had departed, "I might have thought you would refrain from such an extravagant use of your time with so little of it left to plan the wedding in."

Freddie had pointed out that this was her idea, to which Miss Understood replied that, "young Master Blythe has clearly imbibed too much and will have quite the headache in the morning, not that that is any concern of mine."

Lady Darriby-Jones sensed great joy in Lady Alice, compounded enormously when, quite by chance, Alfie arrived back just as pudding was being served at the end of lunch. He went straight to her and gave her a long kiss as she sat at the table.

"That's what I like to see, a union formed from love," one of their friends said, although Manners had rather spoilt the moment by stating in a loud voice that Mr Burrows was doing rather well out of the arrangement.

Torino hastily arranged for another place to be laid, cleverly putting Alfie in a corner position at the table so that nobody was shunted down to make way for him. It was quite crowded, but they only had to fit a bowl of sponge pudding and custard and a single glass for the dessert wine, so he squeezed in well-enough.

"Where have you been?" someone asked from a few places away. "Not sowing your oats, I hope."

"No, sir. I've been doing some research into the Darriby family."

"For your wedding speech, no doubt," came another comment. Alfie decided to let this comment stay without correction, it being too complicated to get into an explanation of what his true purpose had been.

Or purposes, as he stressed to Lady Darriby-Jones immediately after lunch.

"We need a full debrief," Lady Darriby-Jones replied.

"Yes, but to a much smaller audience, eh... Lady Darriby-Jones. Perhaps we should wait until the guests have left. By the way, Torino told me of this surprise party. I understand Miss Understood is responsible?"

"That's correct, but she's taken off for the day, so we just decided to make the most of it."

"Why was Manners here?"

"I don't know how Miss Understood put together this partial guest list; it seems to be totally random in its origin."

As the guests drifted off after lunch, it would seem the opportunity for a thorough debrief by Alfie might soon be upon them; Lady Darriby-Jones remembered Alfie's previous comment about there being something else to consider and was anxious to hear what this other item might be.

However, the guest's departure coincided with Miss Understood's return. She brooked no suggestion of her responsibility in this matter, wanting instead to delve into elaborate half-plans to use the full extent of the grounds around Darriby Hall for the wedding.

"With such magnificent features, Lady Darriby-Jones, I really don't see why we should limit it to the village church and a marquee on the lawn. There are some splendid features, like the ruins of the abbey we could weave into the happy day."

Lady Darriby-Jones was learning that Miss Understood was pretty good at weaving things into things, just that most of her weaving seemed to come immediately undone.

"I have an idea, Miss Un... eh, Miss Stood," Lady Darriby-Jones said when she didn't think she, or anyone else for that matter, could stand a minute more of her 'weaving'. "Why don't you retire to your planning room and write up your ideas so that Lady Alice and I might more easily digest them?"

"Very good idea, Lady Darriby-Jones. Please have Torino send a pot of tea and some biscuits to my room."

"I've actually given staff the rest of the afternoon off, after they've..."

"What? No tea? I must say, I hope you're not planning to give them the day of the wedding off as well? This needs to be the focus of all our minds right now."

"I know," said Maeve, "I'll pop down to the kitchens and make several pots of tea, bringing one to you, Miss Stood."

"That's very kind, Sergeant. Thank you. I find tea a marvellous lubricant for the grey cells." She tapped her head as if a prompt for everyone to 'ooh' and 'aah' about the genius wedding planner, stepping out from the shadows and fulfilling everybody's dreams.

"Right," said Lady Darriby-Jones when the group eventually dwindled to the hard core of the two detective teams late in the afternoon of Saturday. "Right, let's be hearing from you, Alfie, my dear."

"Well," he said, wondering whether to stay seated or stand up to address the collection of amateur detectives before him, "first I need to report my findings on the Archery Murder of 1067."

"You mean you found something about it?" Mrs Robinson asked. "I thought it probably made up."

"Yes, Mrs Robinson, that is my conclusion. I've eventually traced it back to its origin, not in 1067 but to 1844, sad to say because it is a truly magnificent story, reminiscent of the best of historical fiction writers."

"I thought as much," Mrs Robinson said. "Are you able to give us some details?"

"Yes, of course." Alfie took a notebook from his suit jacket pocket and opened it, shuffling between the pages of what seemed like quite extensive notes. "It all started when a Lord Darriby inherited the estate and title in 1840. This would be the current Lord Darriby's great grandfather. He wanted to bring some spice to the family history, which he felt to be a little dull compared to other families who had moved across with William the Conqueror in 1066. He apparently felt that the Darribies, as a clan, hadn't done an awful lot in the almost eight-hundred years since. Lacking the desire to become an explorer or admiral, or some such significant figure in the country, he did have a lively imagination and he used that to write a book, which he called:

The Ancient Happenings of the Darriby Estate

Myths, Legends and True Facts of the Origin of the Darriby Family.

"Unfortunately for all the readers of this single edition book, it contained almost exclusively myths and legends and precious few true facts."

"And," Freddie butted in, "the Archery Murder was one of those myths."

"Exactly, Freddie, and quite a fine one, I'd say. Wouldn't you agree?"

"Oh yes, one of the finest. But that leaves a big question we have to resolve."

"Somebody must have read the book and decided that was the perfect way to carry out the current day murders," Lady Darriby-Jones suggested.

"So, all we have to do is find out how many copies of this book there are, track them down and we have a path to the door of our murderer," Maeve added. "This is exciting, is it not?"

"I have news on that too," Alfie said, illustrating how fine a mind he had, especially when it came to researching into the past. "However, I don't want you to get your hopes up, because ultimately I'm at a dead end."

"How so?"

"I said it was a single edition book. This much I've checked with the publishers, who are still going today. In fact, they are in the very same offices as the earlier Lord Darriby would have visited back in the 1840s. Twelve copies were printed. Yes, that's right, just twelve. Ten were delivered here and held in the library at Darriby Hall. They were destroyed in the fire of 1878. Two were sent to libraries in Oxford. One, the one I've seen, has never been lent out. It's what this library calls their base stock. People can request to read it in the library, but never to take it out."

"So, we can see in the register who has requested to read it?"

"Yes, Mrs Robinson, but unfortunately nobody has made such a request since 1879 when Lord Darriby's grandfather viewed it, having just lost the ten copies in the fire of the previous year. The other has been available for withdrawal but has never been taken out."

"So, a complete dead end, is it not?" Maeve said, feeling distinctly odd being present, but not in uniform, given the nature of these discussions.

"Well, not quite, because there's another twist to this, but equally leading to a dead end. You see, last year, this twelfth book was stolen."

"What?"

"Stolen, whisked off the shelf and never returned. Hey, what's that noise? Is someone there?"

Several people had heard the footsteps but, when they rushed to investigate, there was no one there.

Nobody at all.

Chapter Seventeen

The excitement of chasing someone evidentially listening in to their conversation broke the subject in hand into two distinct halves, that aired and that still to be aired. Cess and Freddie, in particular, charged off around the house to try to track down the illicit listener, although Maeve, Lady Alice and Alfie were also deeply involved. The older cohorts – Smith, Mrs Robinson and Lady Darriby-Jones – were initially involved but later slipped back to the drawing room to consider matters further, Smith feeling awkward about being included in such company and not wanting to sit in the presence of his employer.

"There was something else Mr Burrows wanted to raise with us," Lady Darriby-Jones said, keeping to the formality of surnames in the presence of Smith, one of the household staff, although often involved in aspects of the mysteries Lady Darriby-Jones was involved with.

"What was that?"

"That's the thing, I don't know, Mrs Robinson, because he never got a chance to say about it."

"Shall I go and find him, milady?" Smith volunteered, clearly feeling it more appropriate for him to be involved in a straightforward task, rather than standing around in contemplative mood.

"Yes, that's a good idea, Smith."

Smith returned in fifteen minutes with Alfie in tow; fifteen minutes in which Lady Darriby-Jones' mind worked overtime, sounding out occasional aspects of her thinking with Mrs Robinson, who could only hope to affirm or otherwise her sporadic comments, but unable to see any bigger picture as it slowly, hesitantly emerged in Lady Darriby-Jones' mind.

"Twelve copies, ten destroyed in the fire of 1878. That's what Alfie said?"

"That's correct, Lady Darriby-Jones."

"Twelve minus ten is..." she counted on and came to three.

"No, Lady Darriby-Jones, you have to count on from ten, so you get eleven and twelve; if you include the number ten, that being the number you started with, you'll always get the wrong answer."

"Yes, of course, quite so, quite so. I was distracted, of course. Two copies, one stolen last year. One not viewed for almost fifty years. Interesting stuff, eh, Mrs Robinson?"

"Quite so, Lady Darriby-Jones, but it leaves a mystery that boggles the mind."

. . .

"Ah, Alfie, thank you, Smith, for tracking the bloodhound down. Any luck in finding our interloper, Alfie?"

"None whatsoever, Lady Darriby-Jones," he replied, slumping down into a chair next to her. "My guess is it has to be someone in the house. I know there are lots of entrances to Darriby Hall, but the idea that someone can ease themselves in here without anybody noticing is a little fanciful, I think."

"Yes, one of us," Lady Darriby-Jones replied, almost saying the words as a chant, "one of us, but who, Alfie?"

"It could be one of the staff," Mrs Robinson said, but Lady Darriby-Jones shook her head and said she doubted it.

"Milady, there's almost no possibility it's a member of staff," Smith agreed. "You see, they all worship you, milady. I mean, milady, they wouldn't lower themselves, milady, to listen in, not with how they hold you, milady."

"Yes, quite so, quite so, I'm sure." She felt her blood rising with embarrassment at Smith's comments.

But, also, enormous pride at such a stumbling expression of faith in her.

"Alfie, there's something else I wanted to ask you about."

"You mean from the other day? The time we heard the screams as we came out of the east wing?"

"Exactly."

"Well, I'm glad we have a reduced audience for this next bit, because I really didn't know how to say it in front of her."

"Her?"

"Yes, Maeve, of course, because it's all about her."

"You mean there's something else? Give the others the briefest of backgrounds about how Maeve is related to us, by marriage, of course. While you do that, I want to ponder the problem of who was listening in, so be sure to give me a prod with a cattle stick before you move on to new ground, Alfie."

"Yes, eh..." It was the same problem; what does the intended son-in-law call the intended mother-in-law? But she had no time to think of that. There were more important fish to fry at that moment.

Including who had stolen the book from the library.

All too soon, she had to turn back to Alfie's story-telling. She dragged her mind out of her deep thoughts, but soon became engrossed in what Alfie had to say.

"It all is most strange," he started, "quite the coincidence this next bit. You see, Lady Darriby-Jones, I've told the others about the relationship between Maeve and the Darriby clan, her being something like a third cousin, but on a 'step basis', if you can even get step-cousins.

"But the revelations now go to another scale altogether, because Lord Baritone becomes involved."

. . .

"But, he's dead," Lady Darriby-Jones couldn't help but interrupt, "how on earth can he get involved from the other side?"

"Yes, Lady Darriby-Jones, you're quite right. He was hung before Christmas, hung for murder and kidnap. Let me finish the story please, then perhaps take questions at the end."

"Yes, of course, by all means, Alfie. I'll do my best not to interrupt until you've finished."

Alfie felt like pointing out that waiting until he had finished wouldn't constitute interrupting, but this was just a fleeting thought and he didn't want to distract Lady Darriby-Jones from her deeply contemplative position.

He sensed she was close to breakthrough and didn't want to hold up the process. Instead, he continued with his narration, hoping it might contribute towards the solving of the mystery, although distinctly unsure of how it might do so.

"I suppose the British aristocracy is quite interlinked," he said, to open the next stage. "There are, after all, only so many of them, and there must be many cross relationships all over the place. You know what I mean when I say distant cousins marrying, aunts also being second cousins and so it goes on. Well, just that happened with Lord Baritone and the family that Maeve comes from. To cut to the long and short of it, Maeve Morgan is the heir to Baritone, he having no closer relations. Lord Baritone and Maeve Morgan share great-grandfathers on the Baritone side. Everything he owned was supposed to go to the crown, given that he died without issue, but now along comes an heir, springing from nowhere, and she pockets the lot."

Lady Darriby-Jones couldn't help but 'interrupt' at this point. The prospect of her dear friend Maeve inheriting a fortune was too good to be true.

Except it was true. Alfie wouldn't have raised the subject unless he was certain.

"It's a pity about the earldoms," she said. "It would have been nice if they had been tucked away in the bottom of her Christmas stocking too."

"Why couldn't she inherit?" Smith asked, sort of forgetting his place in his excitement.

"Earldoms have to be passed down through the male line, Smith," Lady Darriby-Jones replied.

"Wrong."

"I beg your pardon, Mrs Robinson?"

"Wrong, at least right, but wrong." Those words from Mrs Robinson made Lady Darriby-Jones relight her beacon of hope.

Hope being that thing deep inside which made you carry on regardless of the odds being stacked against one. Here's how she saw it at that moment:

. . .

If anything, Mrs Robinson knew more than even Alfie, that walking and talking encyclopaedia; her knowledge extended to random selections of information that might be useful once or twice in a lifetime.

"In England, it's largely the case, but not so in Scotland." This made Lady Darriby-Jones' point perfectly; who would keep note in one's mind of the differences between inheritance of titles in England and Scotland? Yes, to how long to boil an egg or the year Darriby Hall was first completed, but the obscurities of inheritance law between different countries of the union?

"And the earldoms are Scottish?" she asked after a silence that seemed to last forever.

"Strathfulton is definitely Scottish." That made imminent sense to Lady Darriby-Jones when she considered the name of her own Scottish estate in the remotest part of the Grampian mountains; Strathvuelen was one of her favourite places in the world. Her mind went to the broad valley of the River Vuelen, the western side of which was positioned Vuelen House standing tall and proud with its tower sticking up towards the heavens.

"I'm sorry, Mrs Robinson. Could you repeat that last bit?"

"Yes, Lady Darriby-Jones, of course. I merely said that the origins of Baritone are a little less well-known. I'd have to look it up." Mrs Robinson stood, looking over at the bookcase lining one wall of the drawing room.

"It will be in the library," Lady Darriby-Jones said, knowing exactly what she was looking for. Mrs Robinson left immediately to collect it.

"Who will tell Maeve about this?" Alfie asked, then added that he thought Lady Darriby-Jones to be the obvious candidate.

"Yes, of course, but I want to have my facts right first."

These were confirmed a few minutes later when Mrs Robinson returned with the copy of *Burke's Peerage*.

"It does seem," she said, "that Maeve Morgan is..."

"What's that I hear about Morgan?" came the forcible voice they all knew too well.

"Mr Manners," Lady Darriby-Jones recovered first, "what are you doing here?"

"I've come about important business that concerned my sergeant. Then, I only hear her name being bandied about the minute I enter the drawing room."

Torino entered the drawing room at that point, slightly put out that Manners had charged in there without waiting to be announced first.

"Mr Manners, milady, the... police officer."

"Thank you, Torino. A Scotch, I think for Mr Manners?"

"Not on... actually, why not?"

. . .

Scotch served and slurped at noisily, Lady Darriby-Jones felt able to continue the conversation.

"Can you tell me what the important matter you have to raise with Sergeant Morgan is, Mr Manners?"

"No, Lady Darriby, this is strictly between me and her, as it were. It's not every day you fire a sergeant for gross insubordination."

"Gross insubordination? I would have thought..."

"I don't care what you think, Lady Darriby, this is police business."

"She'll be in tears," Alfie added.

"So? Perhaps she should have thought about that before tearing into me over lunch. Now, where is she so I can send her on her way?"

Chapter Eighteen

"I must insist, Lady Darriby-Jones, I really must."

"What is it now, Miss Stood?" At least she got the name right, but her presence was tiresome. Surely, she could see that the wedding preparations were bypassing her.

"I don't think you're taking the wedding planning at all seriously. I find myself scratching around trying to make preparations when nobody else has a mind to it."

"I assure you, Miss Stood..." Lady Darriby-Jones knew that she ought to be braver about this; her reluctance to dismiss anyone was causing added difficulties.

"I feel as if I'm standing alone against an army of indifference."

"It's not that, Miss Stood." How do you tell someone that they've been side-lined due to a complete inability to handle the very job you were brought in to do? Lady Darriby-Jones had actually made considerable progress herself with regard to wedding planning. She and Lady Alice had come to an agreement on the date that very morning. Alice had bowed to reason, ultimately accepting her mother's argument to postpone the wedding to the third Saturday in April, the one after Easter. It had helped when she had, that morning, received a telegram from Lord Fork promising a return by Easter.

They had selected bridesmaids and gone for the first dress fitting. Lady Alice had been adamant that the staff handle the catering, rather than calling in a specialist firm.

"They look so smart in their new uniforms," she had said, making Lady Darriby-Jones wonder whether this had always been her daughter's design in choosing new uniforms. She and Alfie had had such a choppy relationship: flaming hot and freezing cold. Could Alice have really seen the ultimate result through all that turmoil?

If it had been Alice's plan all along, it seemed to be working, too. Lady Darriby-Jones had conducted regular surveys of Millie and a few of the other maids, noting the initial horror at the new livery giving way through grudging acceptance and on towards some form of actual appreciation. What had Millie said that very morning when bringing in her pot of tea?

"I suppose we do look distinctive, milady. I have to admit they're not as bad as I first thought. At least Billy thinks they're proper smart."

"Billy?"

"Billy Watson, milady, one of the under-gardeners."

"Ah," she had said, picturing Watson's shaggy head and tanned face. Millie had set her sights high, and so she should.

"Lady Darriby-Jones, are you even listening to me? It's imperative that we have a session immediately to iron out these essential points."

"I, eh, can't right now, Miss Stood. You see, I have to go to Oxford on most urgent business. Smith is just bringing the car around now."

"Could I at least have some time with Lady Alice?"

"She's coming with me, I'm afraid."

"Miss Pitt, then, as the chief bridesmaid? I could also do with going through Master Blythe's duties with him."

"I'm terribly sorry, Miss Stood, but both Cess and Freddie have begged to come with me. We've delayed the trip to accommodate their morning schooling, going the moment Mrs Robinson releases them. We'll find time this evening, I'm sure."

Why couldn't she just tell Miss Understood that her services were no longer required? Did something make her want to keep the middle-aged bumbling lady around?

"Where to, Alfie?" she asked a few minutes later with everybody bundled into the car, Maeve along with Freddie, Cess, Alfie and Lady Alice. "I mean, I know to Oxford, but where specifically?"

"Oh," replied Alfie, "let me think. I've been to so many libraries over the last few days. Yes, that's it, Lady Margaret College. Do you know it, Smith?"

"Lady Margaret College? The ladies' college?" Cess asked with a squeal of delight.

"Yes," Alfie replied, "why the interest?"

"That's where I'm applying, to read medicine. Oh, how exciting is that?"

Except her face fell a moment later.

"What's the matter, Cess?" Lady Darriby-Jones asked, ever sensitive to the younger generation gathered around her.

"It's just... well, when I saw myself visiting Lady Margaret College, I thought I might be dressed in a more grownup way. I hardly look like a prospective student, do I Auntie?"

"You look very smart in your school uniform," Lady Darriby-Jones replied.

"Yes, but not sophisticated and elegant, just a silly schoolgirl."

That's the point at which Freddie took over, explaining that everyone has to start somewhere and being a schoolgirl was nothing to be ashamed about.

"Even the most senior dean at Oxford started as a schoolchild, Cess. You're intelligent and hard-working and have everything to be proud about."

"Can I at least lose my hat somewhere?"

"No," replied Freddie, "go in with your head high, topped

off with your hat, because you deserve to go there and they need to see you in all your splendour."

Lady Darriby-Jones spent the rest of the thirty-minute journey considering the mystery over and over again. There were some vital missing parts she still had to determine, but some, at least, would be sorted out by the visit to the library that held the one remaining copy of the book that seemed to be at the centre of this mystery.

Other parts were still confusing and frustratingly so. Was the person listening in to their conversation yesterday connected with the murder? It could be a coincidence. It could be someone walking in, despite what Alfie and the others thought, either innocently or, for that matter, with serious intent.

She asked herself how she could narrow this person down? Well, there was the visit today, that should move things forward, a little at least.

The library at St Margaret College was much like Lady Darriby-Jones imagined university libraries to be the world over. Lacking the architectural elegance of the library at Darriby Hall, it had a stuffy, studious feel to it with a few students dotted around the place as if picked for the roles by a casting director.

They introduced themselves to the chief librarian, a gushing middle-aged lady who actually curtsied to Lady Darriby-Jones. She started to say only household staff curtsied but decided to leave it there; the librarian's exalted view of aristocracy could only help them achieve their objectives.

"Ah, Mr Burrows, yes, you said you would be back and here you are, sir."

"I wonder, Miss Riddle, whether we might have a look of the single copy you have of the Darriby myth book. By the way, Miss Pitt, here, is a Lady Margaret College hopeful."

"No doubt she would like to be shown around. Miss Gould," she turned to one of the students scattered around the library, "would you be able to spare an hour to show Miss Pitt around?"

"Gladly, Miss Riddle." She shook hands with everybody, then said to Cess that her name was Amy and the best thing she had ever done was to come to Lady Margaret College.

"They're taught to say that," Miss Riddle joked, issuing her words so quickly after Amy's that Lady Darriby-Jones was left with the impression that it was a stock joke dragged out whenever she arranged a visit for a prospective student.

"Can I come too?" Freddie asked, delighted to receive a warm and welcoming smile alongside the comment, "the more the merrier!"

As they left the library, Lady Darriby-Jones heard Cess explaining that she had come straight from the classroom and would have got changed if she had known the destination was her chosen college for Oxford.

"Not to worry," Amy replied, "I came to look around the college myself last year and Mother insisted I come very much as you are. My dress was red, but otherwise very like yours, Cess."

"See, I told you so," Freddie said as they walked through the door to start their tour.

That left a core of people with Lady Darriby-Jones to look over the book on Darriby myths. But Lady Darriby-Jones had another reason for wanting to visit the library where it was held.

She waited until Miss Riddle had dug out the book from a locked cupboard, noting that the keys were on a lanyard attached to her waist.

"Has that always been the practice?" she asked, nodding at the keys.

"Yes, the locked cabinets hold all the valuable or unique books and there's a strict protocol for accessing them, Lady Darriby-Jones."

"Good," she replied. "But, how do you think someone managed to steal the Darriby Myths book, then?"

"Oh, I know exactly how they did it, Lady Darriby-Jones," Miss Riddle replied, "and when it happened too."

Chapter Nineteen

"Well," said Miss Riddle in response to Lady Darriby-Jones' question as to how she knew who had stolen the book, "I don't have a name, but do have a description of her."

"I thought it might be a she," Lady Darriby-Jones replied, "please tell all."

"It's simple. We introduced these rules long before my appointment as chief librarian. That happened in an acting capacity when the then current chief went off to the war. Sadly, he did not return. I was confirmed in this appointment the week after the first day of the Battle of Ypres in '17. But, as I say, the rules were already in place, probably since the turn of the century."

"So, strict control is kept of this key?"

"Yes, Lady Darriby-Jones, but that's not the 'key' to this riddle, if you will forgive the pun. Rather, it's my photographic memory, something I've always had and often think of as a curse rather than a blessing."

"I see, but, in this instance, a blessing, I hope?"

"Very much so, Lady Darriby-Jones. I can give you a complete description of all the visitors we received on the day the book disappeared. Or, more accurately, I should say the night the book disappeared."

"How do you know it was night and how many visitors? I apologise for bundling my questions up in pairs, but I sense this is important."

"That's the thing," she said.

"What's the thing?" Lady Darriby-Jones wondered if Miss Riddle had spent her whole life talking in riddles. Perhaps it went with the name.

"Sense, as in smelling is a sense and is similar to scent, that which is smelt. I'm quite the expert at crossword puzzles, you see."

"You're losing me, Miss Riddle."

"The smell of people is how I can recall what they look like. I associate the smell of someone with how they look and then can forever remember them, just by thinking about the smell."

"Fascinating, Miss Riddle, can I ask what our book thief smelt like, then?" Lady Darriby-Jones hoped she didn't sound too sceptical; the subject interested her enormously, but she also saw the funny side of it.

"Yes, musty, like stale moth balls. It reminded me of someone who was a dragon in the office, or wherever she earned her crust. The point is that nobody around her had the courage to even suggest gently that she gives her clothes, and perhaps her body too, a good airing.

"The courage?" Lady Darriby-Jones replied, sensing it her turn to talk in riddles, "perhaps that's what I lack too?"

"I don't follow," Miss Riddle said. Despite her declared expertise with crossword puzzles, it seemed she wasn't that hot with riddles sent her way.

"I've backed off from having the courage to send someone away recently. Perhaps that might have made a difference. Still, tell me about what this lady looked like, Miss Riddle. Also, how do you know the book was pinched overnight?"

"Oh, that last bit is easy," she replied, "she was the only visitor that day and she 'came back' first thing in the morning but said she had popped in by mistake and left again without looking at anything else. She must have hidden it in one of the cupboards there overnight and then popped out in the morning, walking out with the book in her handbag. What a cheek, I tell you."

They spent twenty minutes perusing the remaining copy of the book written by Darriby's great grandfather, then Lady Darriby-Jones said it was time to go.

"We may have to wait for the tour to finish," Alfie said.

"Blow, I forgot about that. I need to get back pronto."

"Because you know who the murderer is, Mummy?" Lady Alice asked.

"Let's just say I've got one more check to do, but that's got to be carried out at Darriby Hall."

"We could leave Freddie and Cess to get the train back," Alfie suggested.

"No, you see I need them for my final check."

"I'll go and see if I can track them down," Miss Riddle said, then thought of a grander plan and clapped her hands to gain the attention of the students in the library.

"Girls," she said, "we've got a special mission and Lady Darriby-Jones very much needs your assistance."

"Lady Darriby-Jones?" one girl asked, "not the famous detective?"

"Well..."

"We'd love to help. Girls, what are you waiting for?"

"We need to track down two fellow visitors who Miss Gould took off for a tour of the college."

"What do they look like?"

Miss Riddle winked at Lady Darriby-Jones and said leave the descriptions to her. Lady Darriby-Jones cottoned on to her ability to remember detail and nodded in approval.

"The girl is five feet exactly, slight with pigtails and a stubby nose. She's wearing a blue school uniform with a matching blue beret and carrying a mac folded over her left arm. He's taller, maybe five-nine, sandy hair and a face dotted with freckles. He's got the sunniest smile ever and is also in school uniform, although nothing I've ever seen worn around here before. They both smell of..." she paused.

"Yes, Miss Riddle, what do they smell of?"

"Fun, kindness and honesty. Now split off and scour the whole college, girls. Lady Darriby-Jones, I'm sure, will run to a cream tea for your troubles."

"Better than that," Lady Darriby-Jones said, "at a date that's convenient for you, Smith, my chauffeur, will come and collect you in the Rolls and bring you all to Darriby Hall for a slapdash tea and a chat about some of my more interesting cases."

"Well," said Miss Riddle twenty seconds later, "I've never seen a library empty so quickly."

———

"Here's what I want you to do," Lady Darriby-Jones briefed everyone while sitting in the Rolls on the way home. "You, Cess, and Freddie have a critical role to play in this. The others, including me, will be more of a decoy, but I shall be the main communicator, running between you two and the drawing room where Alfie, Ali and Maeve will be talking incessantly about wedding plans. Right, that's the basics. The rest we have to play by ear."

That meant an exhausting afternoon in prospect for Lady Darriby-Jones as the runner between the two parties. She started in the drawing room where Miss Understood met them.

"Freddie and Cess, I do believe you have homework to do."

"But Aunty..." Freddie played his part beautifully.

"No buts, Freddie, you know that Mrs Robinson let you out early this morning so you could go to Oxford. The proviso was that you caught up with all your homework while Cess studies for her entrance exam. Off you two go now and don't let me down."

"Where did you go in Oxford?" Miss Understood asked.

"To St Mar…" Cess started to say, then thought better of it. "To the market for pretty things to wear for the wedding." She realised her second mistake the moment the words left her mouth.

"That's nice. Perhaps you can show them to me?"

"Yes, but not now, Miss Stood. They really need to get on with their schoolwork or I'll have Mrs Robinson to answer to."

"Yes, of course."

"Now," continued Lady Darriby-Jones, "you are going to have the undivided attention of Lady Alice and Mr Burrows for the next hour, plus Maeve as a bonus. I will be in and out as time permits, able and willing to pitch in when I can."

"I see," Miss Understood said, a frown on her face.

"Right, I'll deliver the school contingent to the classroom and be back in a moment. You lot can make a start."

"Perhaps, Lady Darriby-Jones, you could leave the drawing room door open? I find the constant opening and closing quite a distraction as I'm trying to concentrate on the plans."

. . .

That concession meant they had to hush their voices as Lady Darriby-Jones led Cess and Freddie up two flights of stairs to the second-floor landing.

"Here's where we diverge," Lady Darriby-Jones whispered, although two floors up there was no chance of being overheard.

She led them down the passageway, past their own rooms and on to that occupied by Miss Understood.

"Right, in you go, double quick. You remember what we're looking for?"

"The book," said Freddie, far too loudly.

"Hush," said Cess, finger over mouth, "you'll give the game away."

"I'm going back to the drawing room," Lady Darriby-Jones said after easing them into Miss Understood's bedroom.

"Wish us luck," Freddie whispered back.

"We don't need luck, Freddie, we just need to tackle this like a proper forensics job," Cess said loudly, forgetting her own strictures about sound and the way it travelled, bouncing off old stone walls.

Lady Darriby-Jones left them, wondering what it was like to be of an age where everything is fun and exciting. She was lucky in having them around and would be saddened when they eventually grew up and, inevitably, moved on to other things.

. . .

"Ah, Lady Darriby-Jones, there you are," Miss Understood's voice penetrated her various thoughts.

"Yes, Miss Stood, I said I would be along, didn't I?"

"Yes, but the thing is, Lady Darriby-Jones, Lady Alice doesn't know the first thing about plans for her wedding. I really think she should be more engaged, don't you?"

That was a red rag to a bull and Lady Darriby-Jones knew it, setting off alarm bells.

"If you don't need me..." Alice started.

"We all need each other, at least for a while longer. Let's take a step back and calm down a mite. I've just got to pop upstairs for half-a-tick, really and truly won't be long."

Lady Darriby-Jones rose from her seat before the objection could be heard, but not before Alice received a severe reprimand for cheekiness.

Lady Darriby-Jones had one mission to manage, one remaining clue to investigate.

Upstairs, Freddie and Cess had narrowed it down considerably, but not yet found the missing book.

"Well," said Freddie, "if she tries to make a run for it she'll get the soaking of her life, that's for sure." Lady Darriby-Jones looked out of the window and saw the rain slashing down.

"I hope it won't come to charging around after the suspect," Lady Darriby-Jones said, picking up a comb from the dresser and fiddling it through her fingers.

The Mystery of the Wettest Wedding Ever

"If it is her," Cess added, "you see we haven't found the book yet and have searched everywhere."

"Really, everywhere? Can you search again? I need to get back. Miss Understood was curious enough already."

"It didn't help that I almost mentioned the college," Cess added, "that would have completely given the game away."

Back in the drawing room, Lady Darriby-Jones sat down on the chair she had vacated a few minutes earlier, then froze in horror when she saw Miss Understood staring at the comb still in her hand.

"You've found out, haven't you?"

"Yes, Miss Stood. We worked it out. There was really no one else."

"I should have left days ago. Maybe I would have gotten away with it if I hadn't been under your nose the whole time."

"I think that was your big mistake, Miss Stood. Can you tell me two things before Maeve Morgan arrests you?"

"I can't," Maeve said.

"What?"

"I'm suspended and waiting for my dismissal from the service. Mr Manners has gone the whole way this time, has he not?"

"You've got something to tell Miss Morgan, though, don't you, Lady Darriby-Jones?"

"Yes, but how did...?" As Lady Darriby-Jones talked, she rose and rang the bell for Torino.

"Remember, I'm a good listener. I've sneaked around this house listening in to your various attempts at detective work. To be fair, some of them are quite good, but..."

"They caught you, didn't they?" Lady Alice said in a way only Lady Alice could.

"Yes, but a big part of me wanted it to end. Murder, even from forty yards with a bow and arrow, is not a pleasant way to deal with one's fellow human beings. When I was passed over for partnership this last time, I had no other course of action to follow. I had to do something drastic. I thought if I framed Lucy for the murder of her business partner, I could take over the firm."

"Why Peter Park, though?" They all turned to see Lucy Mason, bow in one hand. "I've just come back from the tournament," she explained, "I saw the door open and heard your voices."

"Peter Park was sidling up to you to go into business with him, wasn't he?"

"What? I would never go into business with him, too weak by a long way. Now, Emma Peter is another matter altogether. We're actively discussing about our prospects and expect to do something together when I get back to London."

"Peter Mason," Alice said.

"I prefer Mason Peter," Lucy replied.

. . .

Then, everything happened at once. Torino came to the door and Lady Darriby-Jones asked him to call the police. Just as Torino was leaving for the study and the telephone, Cess and Freddie came down the stairs at record pace, almost knocking Torino over.

"Aunty, we found it, we found the book," they cried. Cess withdrew the book from the pocket of her dress and showed it to the crowd.

"You looked in my bed?" Miss Understood gasped.

"Of course we did. It was the last place on our list."

Chapter Twenty

The third Saturday in April started with a thunderstorm. After hail and light specks of snow, it settled down mid-morning to a relentless pelting, great big drops attacking anyone who dared to go outside.

"What a frightful day," Freddie said, "I've worked like bally-ho these last two months to get ready and now we get it chucking down."

"You've done an excellent job, Freddie," Alfie said, "I think we should go to the church now, lest we be late."

"I think that's unlikely," Lady Darriby-Jones said, "it's still an hour or more to go. Although, I know it to be bad luck to see the bride on the day." She shifted around in her chair to look directly at Freddie, telling him he had done a brilliant job since the school had allowed him to stay for half-a-term, studying with Cess in the morning and working on the wedding afternoons and evenings."

"Thank you, Aunty, it's been fun, but super hard work. Lucy helped out quite a bit, of course."

"We couldn't have done it without Freddie and we couldn't have done it without Lucy," Mrs Robinson announced to those assembled in the drawing room.

"And," said Maeve Morgan, the new Countess of Baritone and Strathfulton, "I'd still be in uniform shackled to Mr Manners without all of you, especially you, Alfie."

"Now we just need God to clear the skies and we'll be in Happy Land."

———

Manners hadn't believed his ears when he had heard about Maeve's elevation to two earldoms, essentially a ticket to every closed door in Britain.

Except for the door that led to Manners' cottage; he had refused all contact. Rumour was he had applied for another position within the Oxfordshire police; others said he had resigned himself, but the owners of that particular rumour went from Happy Land to Distress Land when asked why he was still in his post.

"When are you going to Scotland?" Lady Darriby-Jones asked Maeve at the reception. The rain had stopped, but steam rose from the ground all around the marque that Freddie and Lucy had organised.

"Next week, unless you kick me out earlier, will you now?"

"I wonder what they'll make of a Welsh lady in charge of the estates when they've been so used to a Scottish man?"

"I don't know, but I'm as scared as they come, am I not?"

The Mystery of the Wettest Wedding Ever

"You'll be fine now, Maeve my dear. The Scots are a lovely race; did you know that a lot of them have ancient connections back to Wales? Two Celtic countries fighting for headroom in an Anglo-Saxon world."

"You make it sound so romantic, don't you, Lady Darriby-Jones?"

"Ah, that reminds me of something," she said, "come with me, my dear. Can you see Alfie anywhere?"

"There was talk of them going off soon," Maeve replied.

"All the more reason to rush, then."

They found Alfie and Lady Alice newly changed in their going away clothes.

"Have you come to tell me to look after your daughter, Lady Darriby-Jones?" Alfie asked with a huge smile.

"No, well, yes, of course, but something else, which is why I wanted Maeve here, sorry, the Countess of Baritone and Strathfulton."

"It will take me an age to get used to that name, won't it just?"

"Names, that's what this is all about. You two can't be calling me 'Lady Darriby-Jones' anymore, not now that you're both actually related to me."

"What then, Lady, oh, blow, I almost did it again."

"The trouble is, I've always disliked my Christian name and, unlike Darriby-born stock, I've only got the one to fall back on, as it were!"

"So, what do we call you?"

"I think 'Aunty' might be just right; don't you think?"

"I do... Aunty," said Alfie.

"Can I ask what your first name is... Aunty?" Maeve said.

"You can ask, Maeve, but that doesn't mean I'm going to tell you, now does it?"

"The Mystery of the Missing Name," Alice said, coming in late to the conversation.

"Yes, let it stay a mystery for now," Lady Darriby-Jones replied. "We've had our share of mysteries, have we just not? Now off you two go. I've heard that Freddie and Cess have prepared quite a surprise for when Smith drives you away in the Rolls."

The End

Afterword

Thank you for reading The Mystery of the Wettest Wedding Ever. I really hope you enjoyed reading it as much as I had writing it!

If you have a minute, please consider leaving a review on Amazon or the retailer where you got it.

Many thanks in advance for your support!

The Mystery Of The Polite Man

CHAPTER 1 SNEAK PEEK

Chapter 1 Sneak Peek

*E*very time Lady Darriby-Jones turned the corner from the herb garden to view the front of the house she had married into, she was struck with how handsome her home was. Dating from the reign of Queen Anne, it had both symmetry and ramshackleness, classical proportions and eccentric additions demonstrating the peculiar personalities of a long line of Darriby predecessors. The front façade faced south and the August morning sun put crazy patterns of light and shade across the pale yellow stonework, making a patchwork or a chessboard of her home.

She stopped a moment to take in the familiar view. A bee buzzed to her left; no, not a bee, but the whine of Fingle's taxi as it made off down the drive. Somebody had arrived.

Or somebody had left.

The gravel crunched under her sturdy shoes as she made her way towards a figure standing on the steps outside the front door, the door they barely ever used because it stuck so terribly.

"Darriby," she said when in earshot and saw her husband perched in the doorway. No answer at all, nor on the repeat vocalisation.

"Darriby, dear, what on earth is happening?" She reached the bottom of the steps and looked up fondly at her husband, a man losing several fights. The first was with his weight; easily tackled by letting out his trousers, sadly a regular event now. The second was with his head of hair, or rather lack of it; several retreating blond tufty splodges like a badly mown lawn. The final losing position was with fashion; his choice of suit was from the turn of the century.

Lord Darriby hadn't spent a guinea on clothes since he'd inherited his uncle's wardrobe a quarter of a century earlier. He argued there was little point with so many handsome suits to choose from. Lady Darriby-Jones remembered the outfit he had selected for their wedding day, a Victorian dress coat with a mismatching pair of breeches that ended at the knee and a regular stove pipe of a hat. As for the shoes, suffice it to say that his uncle's nickname had been 'Big Banana Feet'.

"Oh dear, oh dear," Lord Darriby-Jones muttered, whether to his wife of twenty-one years or to himself, she couldn't say.

"Why 'oh dear', dear?"

"She's gone, dear, gone." Well, that solved two things; he was undeniably talking to his wife, although not looking her way, rather staring forlornly down the drive towards the gates half a mile distant, where a motor car now moved silently across the field of view, its hum lost to the steadily increasing distance. And it was someone departing, not arriving.

Now Lady Darriby-Jones had only to determine the object Darriby referred to. She remembered Fingle's taxi, his motor revving unnecessarily over the gravel. Didn't that mad Irishman know that the more you pushed your foot down on gravel, the slower you moved across it; something to do with someone's Law of Motion on Driveways.

Or did that particular magazine article cover tactics at golf? She resolved not to travel first-class on the trains anymore; they had such giddy magazines, full of useless claptrap, available in the first-class waiting room.

"Dear, who exactly has gone?" She raised her voice, feeling not quite the lady she'd become since marrying Lord Darriby-Jones.

"Why, Miss Fire, of course."

"Miss Fire?" She felt she should know anyone with such a distinctive name. She briefly imagined Miss Fire attending the symposium in revealing costume to entertain the gentlemen. Then it came to her. "Oh, dear, you mean Miss Fryer?"

"That's what I said, dear."

It took another dozen 'dears' to get the facts established, six from Lady Darriby-Jones and half-a-dozen from her husband.

Miss Fryer was the latest in a long line of secretaries to Lord D-J. The last eight had left because of the onerous work conditions at Darriby Hall. Now it seemed Miss Fryer was the ninth, although Lady Darriby-Jones didn't want to jump to conclusions.

"Why did she leave, dear?" she asked her husband, taking the twelve steps three at a time to stand next to him.

He mumbled his reply, invoking a 'don't mumble, Darriby' response, but softened by taking his big hairy hand in her chubby little one.

"She said she wasn't going to cut up slugs. She waved this paper in my face and said it was her job description and it said nothing about slugs. How can that be, dear?" He drew his wife to him, thinking how much chubbier she was than the waif-like creature he'd stood at the altar with.

He liked chubby, so he pulled her towards himself, knocking against the Darriby Duck on its plinth in the process. Darriby Duck rocked slightly, looking as if it would totter and fall, likely smashing against the granite steps, but Lady Darriby-Jones's rather ample bottom moved in, steadying the stone duck while attempting to steady her husband's shattered nerves.

"It's alright, Darriby dear, we'll simply find another one. Don't worry, it will work out." These words were meant for reassurance but failed miserably. Lord Darriby-Jones took a step back (producing more pressure on Darriby Duck, but Lady Darriby-Jones's bottom was firmly in place now), and wailed his next words.

"How will I ever be ready for the symposium, Jonesy? Everything I've worked for?" As the problems had elevated themselves, Lord Darriby-Jones had moved on from the 'dear' stage, on to his interpretation of the half of the surname she'd brought with her on that happy occasion twenty-one years ago come September 12th. It had been a condition her father had set on approving her move into the aristocracy and before the rather impressive dowry had changed hands. Evan Jones, her dearly departed father, had sought a permanent link with the next best thing to royalty, securing the 'Jones' name amongst the aristocracy in one simple move, one contract drawn up and a pot of money moving from one healthy bank account to a rather overdrawn one.

Surprisingly, for such a mercantile start to a marriage, it had been an excellent one. Politeness had developed into fondness and fondness had steadily progressed to a form of love, at least that is how a marriage guidance counsellor would see it, not that they had ever needed to seek advice on their marriage.

"Never fear, dear, I will this very day locate a new secretary for you. See if I don't."

"You will, dearest...dear?"

"I will. I shall go this very morning to Oxford to procure the best there is." She was well aware of her weakness for impulsive offerings, but, surely, she would find someone in that heaving mass of spires and churches? Besides she made a sudden determination to order her husband a new suit for the limacology symposium coming up in October and there was no better place for suit procurement than the rather proper *Salensby, Grist and Partridge.* She looked at the watch, pinned upside down to her jacket, sister-in-hospital style, although Lady Darriby-Jones had never worked a day in her life. She could just catch the 11.43 if she got her skates on.

There was time for a quick cuddle first. She would telephone the station and ask the station master at Darriby Halt to keep the train a minute or two; the man owed her a favour after locating his missing daughter just last year, tracing her all the way to the travelling circus and snatching her back from the clutches of a wicked clown who, it turns out, the police were rather interested in. No doubt the man was raising the prison roof right now with his comic antics and slapdash act.

She rather liked her cuddles.

"I'll go now," she said between the kisses she had to stand on tiptoe to achieve. "Catch the morning train...Oxford...secretary...telephone...tell Smith..."

Just then, they heard the swishing sound of someone swiping at undergrowth. They knew the sound and what produced it. They made to detach themselves before Lady Alice, the only offspring from their union, turned the house corner on her march to, or from, the stables.

"Got you, evil weed," she shouted in triumph.

"Morning, dear," Lady Darriby-Jones called across the rising heat of the day.

"Got you good and proper."

"Going riding?" A silly question because she was dressed for riding with shiny long boots polished by Sam, the groom who worshiped Lady Alice, together with jodhpurs, jacket and tie and riding hat.

Lady Alice, 'Ali' to her friends (who numbered rather few, not that she cared) walked directly past her parents standing together at the top of the steps, not seeing them at all. It wasn't even a case of 'out of sight, out of mind', Lady Darriby-Jones considered; they were plainly visible yet totally invisible to their nineteen-year-old daughter.

"Good morning, milady, station is it today?" Smith seemed out of a bygone era, dressed smartly in his chauffer's uniform, holding the door to their 1910 Silver Ghost and smiling inanely as he greeted his employer.

"Yes, Smith," she replied, then added on impulse, "Tell me, Smith, how long have you been with us?"

"That depends, milady."

"Depends on what?"

"What year it is now, milady."

"Why, it's 1924, of course." She watched him count with his fingers a long while, drumming them against his trousers. Then he gave up on the calculation.

"I was a nipper when I started here, milady. Must have been 1863 or thereabouts." It was now Lady Darriby-Jones's turn to exercise her mind with simple arithmetic. She did so as the car made its gradual passage down the drive. No hurry, for the morning train would wait.

"That's seventy-nine years you've been a resident here at Darriby, three times longer than me," she eventually pronounced through the speaking tube. "No, that can't be right. Fifty-eight years, Smith."

"Fifty-eight and counting, milady." Smith slammed the

brakes on, throwing Lady Darriby-Jones forwards from her seat. "Sorry, milady, there was a cat."

"What type of cat?" she asked before she could stop herself.

"A black one, milady. Did you see it, milady? If you didn't, then it don't count as bad luck, milady. That's the rule we always said, milady."

"What black cat, Smith? You must be imagining it." Only she had seen a fleeting black object, darting from left to right across the single-track road.

"Here's the train, ready and waiting for you, milady."

Get your copy of this gripping murder mystery at all good retailers.

A LADY DARRIBY-JONES MYSTERY

THE MYSTERY OF THE POLITE MAN

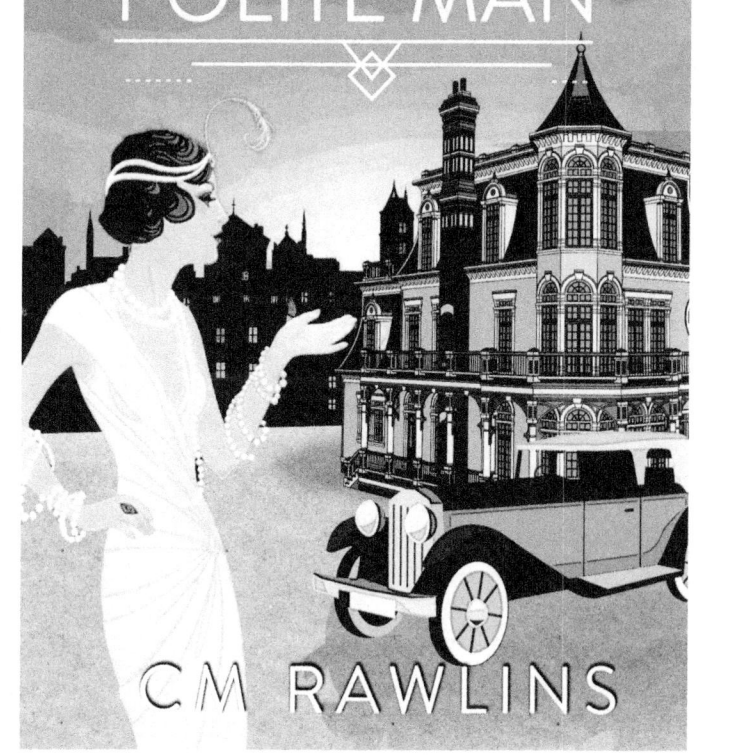

CM RAWLINS

Also By CM Rawlins

A Lady Darriby-Jones Mystery Series

The Mystery of the Polite Man (Book 1)

The Mystery of the American Slug (Book 2)

The Mystery of the Back Passage (Book 3)

The Mystery of the Murder that Wasn't (Book 4)

The Mystery of the Miss Cess Pitt (Book 5)

The Mystery of the Bag of Bones (Book 6)

The Mystery of the Sudden Demotion (Book 7)

The Mystery of the Missing Misses (Book 8)

The Mystery of the Royal Rogue (Book 9)

The Mystery of the Mothering Sunday (Book 10)

The Mystery of the Christmas Crackers (Book 11)

The Mystery of the Wettest Wedding Ever (Book 12)

Newsletter Signup

Want **FREE** COPIES OF FUTURE **CLEANTALES** BOOKS, FIRST NOTIFICATION OF NEW RELEASES, CONTESTS AND GIVEAWAYS?

GO TO THE LINK BELOW TO SIGN UP TO THE NEWSLETTER!

https://cleantales.com/newsletter/

Printed in Great Britain
by Amazon